GRACE

Many people fall from grace because Grace is the most unstable destination to ever exist. It remains a popular vacation resort however. Grace— unlimited money, power, success; the ability to do whatever you want to do in life and not have to answer to anybody. Being your own boss, basically printing your own money. Living life on your terms. Grace is controlled by the number one law of reality: If you're still alive, you still have the burden of living.

A tear trail flowed from Ashlon's eyes to the bottom curve of her chin. It accumulated there, seemed to pause for a second as if checking for final instructions; and after a moment of finality, it fell in the form of a tear drop onto the open pages of her Bible. It was 8 P.M. on a Tuesday night, and unlike many of the days of her past... nothing was wrong for once in her life, not a single thing.

She had everything a woman could dream of, and due to that fact, she was the most afraid that she had ever been. She had a man who she loved and who returned that love. One who was slow to anger and quick to accept fault whenever it occurred. A man who was determined to get it right, and who forcefully fought to keep their marriage strong and healthy. Her career was perfect, her family healthy, she had a loving husband and had overcome so many things to finally be in that position, and she was in tears because she was afraid.

Her fear was that she wasn't good enough to keep her blessings. Her fear was that she was living a dream that maybe she wasn't as deserving enough to keep. She had never experienced happiness on that level, so it was something that she didn't know how to completely handle. The only thing that she knew worked every time was prayer, and she made sure to go in deep prayer each day so that God knew that she didn't take anything for granted.

"God I beg of you for forgiveness for any sins I may have committed either knowingly or unknowingly. I beg of you for a clean spirit, for clear direction, and for a better understanding of my own value. Lord my life changed so fast that I'm just scared, and I pray to you that you send me a sign to show me that it's all ok. I went from lost to being a boss God, and I just don't want to take anything for granted. If it's an assignment you want of me, please make it clearer to me so that I don't miss it. I love the way you've moved in my life Father God, and I pray that you continue to use and move in me and my family's life. God please, I pray to you in the humblest manner possible."

Devin stopped in the doorway to the bedroom and listened to her pray without interrupting.

"God I pray that you keep me and my family safe from the dangers of the world. I pray that you keep us together and walking in your vision. Father God I thank you for the deliverance of addiction, and for the delivery of your touch onto our lives and souls. I thank you for the gift of family Father God, and I pray that you reveal to me how to be the best woman I can possibly be for my husband, his daughter and mine. Thank you God. In Jesus Christ's name I pray. Amen."

Devin closed his eyes and took a soft breath, careful not to interrupt or startle her. That had been the 3rd time that week that she'd been sending up a similar prayer regarding the family. It touched his heart every time, but that time he couldn't take it anymore; he had to reassure her that everything was going to be ok. He walked into the room with a fresh smile on his face.

"Hey baby... What you doing?"

"Oh... Just sending up some prayers. That's all. I love you Devin." She said as she closed her Bible and reached to place it on the table top.

Devin sat beside her and placed one of his palms on the back of her hand. "I listened to your prayer Ashlon... I just want you to know that we're going to be just fine. I'm not going anywhere, and I plan to love you until I take my last breath. When I married you a year ago, I meant it; and I have no plans on changing."

Ashlon gave a weak smile. She heard him but she knew that wasn't what her prayer was about. She had no reason to ever question whether he loved her or not, but every reason to beg God to keep protection over their union. Ashlon knew that with Devin being a public figure and major rap star, that he was exposed to a thousand times the amount of threats that a normal black male was faced with on a daily basis. She would pray until her last breath if her prayers were going to keep them together as a family. She would never lose track or faith.

"Baby... I know... I just love you, and I'm asking God to keep it that way."

"I understand that... But I do want you to know that I'm not going anywhere love. I appreciate and adore you, and I'll never stop with the types of feelings I've accumulated for you. I won't leave our family, and I'm doing the best that I can possibly do not to let you down as your husband." He wiped her tears away as he talked to her. It was an emotional moment, and as he spoke, he thought about some of the advice that his father had given him and adjusted his approach.

He stopped talking, then reached for the Bible and flipped through it until he found what he was looking for. He pressed his pointer finger against the crisp texture of the paper and read it aloud.

"Ephesians 5:28 reads... In the same way husbands should love their wives as their own bodies. He who loves his wife loves himself." Devin showed her the scripture he was reading and looked into her eyes, needing her to feel and understand what he was saying. "Baby I gave up alcohol and drugs simply because I didn't wanna shorten any of the days I'm able to spend time with you. Before you I didn't wanna live another hour, and since falling in love with you, I can't find enough hours in a day to keep my eyes open. I wake up early every morning just to stare at you for a few minutes. The same way some people wake up and stand on the porch to enjoy the sunrise, I rise up in the morning to show appreciation to the star of my eyes. Baby I love you, and I love me because you love me. I love me and I love you just as deep just because we are one. Please know this baby."

Ashlon nodded her head and tried her best to suppress a big grin. Devin laid back on the pillow and Ashlon lay her head against his chest. Hearing him reassure her in his own words made her feel more deserving of the life she had. There was still a tinge of doubt present, but she knew that she was going to fight to get that spirit away from her. It couldn't be anything but the devil bothering her at that point. It had been so many let-downs and disappoints happening in her life that the very moment that everything was perfect was the moment when she was the most afraid. She made a vow to work on blocking out all doubt so that she could enjoy her amazing life.

"I love you Devin." She whispered as she closed her eyes and wrapped her arm over his chest.

"I love you too baby." He said as he wrapped his arm across her body and held her close. "Remember this too... worry is just a misuse of your imagination. I want you to stop worrying so much and start living."

It was a phrase that she could never forget— words that only Devin was able to assemble. She exhaled what felt like an entire shipment of stress and told herself that it could no longer occupy her body. She was going to change her mindset going forward and wasn't going to let anyone make her feel guilty about her blessings.

Besides, she thought to herself... What's the worst thing that could happen? All of the horrible stuff had already happened in both of their lives, so the only thing left was to go up from there. She prayed every day, and she wasn't a bad person, so it was time for her to quit expecting the bad stuff to happen; that had to be a trick of the devil.

Even though she told herself that, the more she lay against him, the more her worrying started flaring back up. The devil just refused to allow her to be happy, but she was going to fight for it. She put it in her mind that she was going to get help from their Pastor when she woke up in the morning. She needed to put that demon to rest so she could live.

OG

Devin's father had been locked up for so many years that it had taken him quite a while to adjust back to the normal routine of society. He had been released for a year at that point, and still got nervous whenever a white person spoke to him, and still panicked whenever he saw a police officer or anyone else wearing a uniform. He had post traumatic stress syndrome.

Despite him jumping at the slightest noise, and keeping a knife in his right pocket out of habit, he still loved the life that his son and daughter in law had provided for him. He had a brand new Jaguar truck, a posh apartment with floor to ceiling windows located downtown Atlanta, and he had a job at Devin's record label managing artists and making sure that they handled their business.

He still couldn't believe how great his life was going after spending so many years on the wrong side of the law. His life had turned into something greater than his wildest dreams. He knew that he would have to shake the mental confines of prison if he wanted to completely enjoy it, and that was something he had been working on. His phone rang while he was doing push-ups in his living room.

"Hello?" He was waiting on the other party to reply, but when the phone rang again he realized that he hadn't answered it correctly. He was still learning. He looked at the phone for a brief second and thought about it, then pressed the answer button harder.

"Hello!?" He said louder, as if that had something to do with it.

"Dad you aight?" Devin said with a slight chuckle in his voice.

OG was breathing hard from the push ups, but smiling from ear to ear from hearing his son's voice on the phone. He was truly happy and couldn't ask God for anything greater than what he'd been given.

"I'm good son. Why you ask that?"

"You answering the phone screaming. You trippin over there Pops."

They both laughed– a rare moment because Devin was so busy handling business and trying to stay relevant in the ever-changing landscape of the rap game. It had been hard for him to be relevant when he'd given up so many vices. They had been the very vices that had turned him into a rock star to begin with. The fact that he was changing his life and making an effort to live for God was making him find other avenues to keep his revenue afloat. It was the purpose of his phone call.

"Pops. It's a rapper named Black Barbee who I wanna bring to our company. I've been reaching out to her for months now on Instagram, and she just finally responded to me."

"She crazy for just responding son. You're Q Money Mack! Who wouldn't–"

"Dad listen please." Devin said as he exhaled. "This lady has 1.5 million followers on Instagram and she's doing her thing independent. She doesn't even need a major record label behind her because she's making so much money on her own, but she still decided to reply to me. So I need you to go to her performance tonight at 1 A.M. and see what she's talking about. Do whatever you can to sign her Pops. We need her."

OG was excited that his son was trusting him to do so many things under the record label. He'd never had a real job before, so it was such a welcomed change that he made sure to do his job diligently.

"Ain't no problem Q Money. Where she performing at?"

"At the Diamond Palace strip club."

OG smiled because he knew he was about to be able to enjoy his entire night. He was about to get a good visual dose of some fine ass women while still gaining his son's trust by doing the job he had been appointed to handle.

"I got you son. I'll let you know what happened in the morning. Get you some rest, I know you're tired."

Devin laughed. "I don't know how you knew... but it's definitely true. I'm about to lay besides my wife and clear my mind of the hassles of the word. I appreciate you Pops. Be careful tonight."

"Careful? You know I got this handled son. I'll talk to you later."

"One."

OG looked at the time and saw that he had only a couple of hours to get ready for the performance. He was ready to introduce himself as the lead A&R for Mack Money Records. His plan was to make his son proud and have Black Barbee ready to sign that contract by the morning, and he was going to try to make that happen by all means.

BLACK BARBEE

"Tory are you taking me to the club tonight?"

Tory shot a menacing scowl, displaying a look of disgust across his face. "That's the only fuckin thing you care about. The damn club."

"That's not true Tory, you know I got a show tonight. If it wasn't for that I wouldn't even go. You know we need this money. I'm doing this for us." Barbee said as she stared at her man hoping he would understand.

Tory got off of the sofa and grabbed a pipe off of the kitchen counter. "Well the shit won't be here when you get back. Just letting you know." Tory said as he started walking towards the bedroom.

"Wait Tory! No! Don't be like that!" Barbee yelled as he continued to walk. "Tory! Stop playing with me!"

"Who the fuck you screaming at bitch? I said what I said and I meant it!" You're a good looking woman, so you can get the shit again, fuck you!"

"No nigga fuck you! I won't let you treat me like this Tory, fuck that! I'm the one who paid for it! Give it to me!"

"Well you better come get a hit right now, because I'm going to smoke it all up while you're out flirting with these niggas in the streets!"

"Tory! Ok well just come with me. I don't wanna smoke before the show baby, you know that. Just come with me." She said as she put her hands around his. "Please baby?"

Tory frowned and stared at her whiled she begged him to come support her at her club performance.

"You won't have to pay anything baby, and they're going to give me some money tonight for performing."

"Oh yea? How much?" Tory asked as he started considering it and thinking about the outcome.

"They're giving me $3,000 tonight." Barbee said with an excited look on her face.

Tory's eyes widened when he thought about what he could do with that amount of money.

"Shit... aight fuck it, I'm going." Tory said as he carefully placed the pipe on the bed.

"You leaving it?" Barbee said as she stared at the pipe wide-eyed.

Tory glanced at it and seemed to be lost in thought for a moment. "Well... we definitely don't wanna get caught with that shit. So either we hit it now, or save it for when we get back."

Barbee felt her throat tighten up as she stared at the crack pipe. She was only 22 years old and seemed unable to shake her crack cocaine addiction. She thought about the millions of people on social media who looked up to her and admired her because of her beauty, and about the legions of fans who showed up to her shows to support her music... She loved the fact that they loved her like that... But the only thing she loved was crack cocaine.

She felt her heart beat faster while staring at the pipe, but knew that she needed to go handle her show before engaging in the drug. She knew she wouldn't be in the best mind to perform while under the influence of such a deeply complex drug. She swallowed hard and shook her head. "Ok baby. You're right. I'm ready.

Let's get out of here. You know the rule we have... No matter what... We have to keep it together in front of the public."

Tory smiled and nodded his head. "That's my baby. You ready?" All he could think about was collecting the money from Black Barbee's performance. Had he known she was getting paid that much from her shows, he would have tried to get her a show set up for every single day.

"I have to put my make-up on and I'll be ready."

"Aight then... well I'll be in the car waiting on you. Hurry up."

"Wait Tory." Barbee said as she stared at his dirty t-shirt and basketball shorts. "You going like that?"

"Like what?" He looked down and looked back up with a confused expression.

"Like... you don't wanna change your shirt? Maybe put on a pair of jeans? You know you'll be on stage with me right? People take a lot of pictures, and this will be all over social media..."

"Shit and what you saying? You ashamed of me or something?" Tory was getting angry all over again.

"Baby... I'm just saying... It was you who told me I– well... we... needed to make sure to preserve our image. I just wanted us to be–"

Tory sighed. "You're right Barbee. How about I stay here tonight, and I'll get a haircut and get my wardrobe correct so I can be with you front and center for your next event. What do you think about that?"

Barbee shrugged. "Baby I don't mind you coming tonight. I'm sorry if I–"

Tory grabbed the pipe off of the bed and handed it to her. "You don't have to apologize Barbee. I'm not going to smoke it up. Here..."

Barbee looked him in the eyes for a brief moment, trying to see if he was trying to trick her, but her heart was beating so fast over the fact that he wasn't threatening to smoke up her drug of choice that she didn't even care.

"No, it's ok... I trust you Tory... Baby I love you. I trust you. I'll leave it here."

"No... because I don't even trust myself. Here." He placed the crack pipe in her hands and reached in his pocket and grabbed the keys to his car. He handed them to her also.

"Wow... You're going to let me drive your car?" She was beyond shocked. Even though she was the one who co-signed for it, he never let her drive it because the car was her pride and joy.

"It's our car baby." Tory said as he placed the keys in her hand. He leaned in and kissed her and went to lay in the bed.

"Baby thank you." Barbee said as she smiled at the man of her dreams. "Thank you for trusting me."

"No... thank you for loving me Barbee. I'll be waiting on you. Put the pipe in the trunk of the car in my shoebox, that way I won't have access to it. I'll see you when you get back."

Barbee was so excited she could barely contain herself. She hurriedly went to the bathroom to apply her makeup before her boyfriend decided to change his mind. She was going to rock that show with all of the confidence in the world, simply because her man had finally shown confidence in her. It cheered her soul up, and she was wearing one of the brightest smiles she'd worn in a very long time.

She'd had a lot of dark days in her life, despite her being one of the most beautiful public figures to walk the earth— nobody knew the depths of pain and the severity of the nightmares she'd been forced to live behind the scenes. She finished applying her make-up and hurried out of the house. She couldn't wait to bring her boyfriend back the $3,000 from her performance.

❦

The club parking lot had so many cars parked that it looked like the largest car dealership in the city. Butterflies bounced against her chest, and her emotions ran high as she drove to the back of the club and parked in her private, reserved space. Her hands shook as she tried to dial the club promoter's phone number. She was so nervous that she dropped her cell phone on the floor. She unfastened her seat belt and reached down to pick her phone up.

When she climbed back up, she was a police officer pull around behind her with his lights on. She figured he was the security, and felt a tinge of relief know that she would have security escort her into the club, and prayed that the same security was going to escort her back out when it was time to go. She didn't have anybody who had her back except her boyfriend, but he never accompanied her to her events; and always gave excuses when it was time to do so.

The officer parked his car and got out, and Black Barbee opened her door and prepared to greet him. Her heart got stuck in her throat when the officer drew his service pistol and aimed it at her.

"Don't move or I'll shoot! Put your hands up so I can see them! Don't move!" The white officer was furious and she couldn't figure out what the reason was.

She kept her hands up so that he could see them, and it wasn't even a few seconds later that another officer drove up with his lights turned on as well. It was dark behind the club, and nobody was there except her and the two officers. She feared for her life as she thought about all of the police shootings that had taken place across the country. She was afraid that they were going to kill her, or that they were nasty and evil men who would rape her and still take her to jail. She was vulnerable at that moment and didn't know what else to do except follow their instructions.

The first officer remained with his gun aimed while speaking to the second officer. The driver of the second police car nodded his head and pulled out his weapon as well, then walked up to the driver's side window slowly with the gun drawn.

"What did I do officer?" Barbee asked as her body shook as if it was 2 degrees outside and she was stark naked.

"Slowly... I want you to step out of the vehicle. Keep your hands up! Slowly... Step out of the vehicle."

Barbee slowly climbed out of the car as asked. She was so nervous that she was about to use the bathroom on herself.

"Turn and face the car and put your hands behind your back. Slowly!" The officer yelled, and the first officer got closer to them with his pistol still aimed at her head.

Her cell phone rang, and it made everyone jump, the second officer almost pulled the trigger, but caught himself when realizing that it was a phone ringtone and seeing that his life wasn't in any type of danger. She put her hands behind her back and the second officer ran up and put his handcuffs on her immediately. The first officer ran up and forcefully pressed her head against the window of her car.

"Ouch!" She yelled. He was hurting her and seemed not to have any regards towards her pain.

The first officer swung her around, almost tossing her to the ground. "I've gotten a report of a stolen car. The owner said he saw you buy drugs and pulled out his phone to film you, and you got angry, pulled a gun on him and made him give you his phone and his car. Are there any drugs in this vehicle ma'am?"

"No sir."

"What?"

"No sir!" Barbee yelled back at the officer.

"So you don't mind that we're bringing a K-9 dog, and you can just sit in the back of my police car while we handle that little search. You better hope like hell that you're telling the truth." The officer said as he walked her to his car.

A third police car pulled up transporting the K-9. The officer got out and put a leash on the the drug sniffing dog and walked up to the blue Dodge Challenger that Barbee was driving. He walked around the car slowly, giving the dog a chance to sniff out any types of drugs. The dog stopped when he got behind the car by the trunk, squatted down and took a piss.

"Find drugs Mike." The officer spoke gently to the dog as he urinated. Mike got back up and walked back around the car again without barking. The officer looked at the other officer, and he shrugged. A voice sounded on his CB, as it was his contact at the precinct calling him back with the results from running the tag that he'd called in.

"I have a 2017 Dodge Challenger, blue, registered to a Barbee Hatherway. Insurance and registration both valid."

The first officer took a deep breath and shook his head. "Fuckin assholes playing on the phone." He went and got back in the car, angry for wasting his time.

The second officer walked back to his car and opened the door. "Hey... Do you have driver's license on you?"

Tears flowed down Barbee's face as she nodded her head.

"Where is your license?"

"In my right pocket." She said as she sobbed.

He felt like the asshole of the century, and guilty of being one of the reasons that black people didn't trust white police officers. He pulled her out of the car and took her handcuffs off as he watched the other officers disappear into the darkness as if nothing happened. "Let me see your license."

He watched her arm shake out of fear as she reached into her skin tight jeans and pulled her ID out. She handed it to him, and he read the name that the vehicle was registered to. *Barbee Hatherway*. He handed her license back and took a deep breath.

"Barbee. Please accept my apology. Apparently someone has it out for you, so I want you to be careful out here. Someone perhaps tried to frame you I'm guessing, or set you up; I'm not sure who your enemies are, but be careful. You have a good night." The officer tilted his hat and watched as she walked away silently.

He drove off into the darkness to join his other co-workers.

Barbee stood in the darkness with tears flowing down her face. His words hurt her to her core, and she couldn't believe that the man that she would do anything for would go to such extreme circumstances to try to hurt her. She had been moving so fast in the bathroom doing her make-up that she had left the crack cocaine and pipe on the sink at the house. She had been so eager to please him that she'd saved her own life in the process. She was thankful that God put his hand out in her time of need and sent angels in the midst of her decision making. It was nobody but God that had helped her overlook the crack cocaine and send her out the house with a smile on her face.

She picked the phone up and saw that the promoter had been calling her. It was almost time for her performance, and she was ready to turn up. She had an entirely new song on her heart that she was going to perform, and she couldn't wait to grab that microphone.

LIKA

She finally had the life that she dreamed of. She had the man of her dreams- one who took care of her mentally, financially, and physically; and one that she *wanted* to be a complete woman for. It was easy for a man to want a woman to be a certain way, but only the right man would make a woman want to be that wanted way.

She wanted it.

She'd cooked a meal suitable for a king, and was fixing his plate while singing along with Ella Mai's smooth voice as it slipped through her portable speakers. Her newborn son was sleeping against his father's bare chest, and his father had fallen asleep on the sofa while trying to get his child to go to sleep. It was the type of picture she could only have dreamed of having, but some type of way it was really happening for her in real life.

Every moment with her new family felt like Christmas Eve, and she was just overwhelmed with excitement. She went and kissed her man on his face until he opened his eyes.

"Dinner's ready... I made your plate." She said with a smile on her face.

He smiled back at her, his smile a turn on, and his presence needed and wanted more than anything she'd ever needed in her life. All she could do was thank God for the situation he'd placed her in. It was the highest point she'd ever been in in her life.

"Alright... Just give me like ten more minutes baby." He whispered in his husky voice.

Lika smiled and sat beside him at an angle so that she could lay her head on his stomach beside their child. She grabbed her iPhone and took a selfie of the three– the ultimate photo of perfection; and she posted it on Instagram and Facebook with the hashtag #3daHardWay. She smiled as the picture immediately started getting likes. She had a thousand likes on Instagram in the first 15 seconds, and the comments ranged from heart eyes to hug emojis to smiles to jealous comments of other women wishing they could also be in the same situation in their lives.

While she was pressing the like button on one of the comments, her daughter walked into the living room.

"Mom." She said as she stood by the television.

"Yes Angel?"

"Did you make me a plate?"

"You can make your own plate baby. Go ahead." Lika said as she went back to replying to a comment under her post.

Angel stared at the three of them laying on the sofa and felt left out. She was happy that her mother was happy, but didn't understand why she never received that type of love and attention that her new brother was receiving. It seemed like the only reason she got attention was because of who her father was instead of getting it because of what her heart was.

She walked into the kitchen and saw two already made plates sitting on the table, along with two cups of fruit punch. She grabbed the carton of fruit punch that was sitting on the table and was disappointed when she realized that it was empty. Her disappointment quickly escalated to anger when she remembered that she was the reason that her mother had been able to buy the food in the first place.

Her mom was all happy over this new man, but the reality was that he didn't have a job, and neither did he do anything besides sleep and hold the baby, and spend the money that had been generated by her father's hard work, sweat, and tears. She grabbed a paper plate and went to the stove to get a piece of the tilapia that she saw on the plates on the table, but didn't see any. Instead, there was only broccoli, roasted potatoes, rice, and creamed spinach.

"Mom where did you put the rest of the tilapia?" Angel asked as she opened the door of the oven only to find it empty.

"Oh baby, I ran out of tilapia. I thought you were sleeping since it was so late. If I would have known you were up I would have went to the store and bought more."

"Sleeping? Mom I hadn't eaten anything... I was waiting on you to cook..."

"Well baby I taught you how to make you something to eat. Why didn't you just make you some tuna earlier if you were hungry?"

Angel sat the paper plate down in disbelief. She couldn't believe her mother was treating her like that, as if she wasn't even a member of the household. She walked back into her room and locked the door. Her father had bought her a cell phone, and she was about to put it to good use. She no longer wanted to stay with her mother, and she was about to let it be known. There was never any food in the house for her, and it was always as if she was a huge inconvenience. She was going to go to where she was loved and wanted.

DEVIN

After talking to his father and giving him instructions regarding the signing of Black Barbee, he'd found himself in the midst of a deep conversation with his wife. He loved moments like that because it was such a deep learning experience for the both of them. It was unlike anything he'd ever experienced in life— it was a chance to learn a woman from the inside out, mentally and spiritually.

"Baby... Why do men cheat?" Ashlon asked as she lay against her husband's warm body.

Devin thought about it for a second before answering. He knew he could talk to his wife the way he would talk to a male best friend if he had one. He could be honest and free to express his opinions without her being mad or taking offense to things that he said. She knew that he loved her, and there was never a moment that she questioned it. She was learning that the more she was able to learn about the male race, the better she was able to love him; and the less things were a mystery.

"Well... It's a few reasons why men cheat love. For starters... you have some men who just like certain sections of relationships."

"Sections?"

"Yes. They like the courting process, the feeling of making a woman smile genuinely, the feeling of a woman feeling like they're the perfect man for them. The feeling of when they touch her for the first time, the satisfaction the woman gets from their first encounter... That first hug, first kiss, first time holding hands... The first emotions are the sharpest, because it's one of the only times a man sees a woman for who she is minus the flaws; and vice versa. We are flawed as people, both men and women are... and for this reason, once we learn more about the opposite sex's flaws, the more we tend to push away and seek newness again. Men more than women though, simply because of the ratio of women to men."

Ashlon absorbed his words without questioning them. She just listened and tried to understand even when his answers didn't make sense. She understood that just because his answers didn't make sense to her didn't mean it was her job to argue or debate it. After all, she was the one seeking the answers.

"The other reasons men cheat... some men at least... It's based on discovery."

"Discovery? Like discovering who they want, or discovering who they are?"

"Like discovery... Meaning... When a young man discovers that different vaginas feel differently, they never stop trying to discover it. Meaning... once they begin this pattern, they stick to this pattern for years. They end up on a life long journey of wine tasting, yet destroying the trust of many women through the course of their hobby."

"Why don't they just be honest and tell the women what it is up front?"

"Because they know it slims the chances that they get a chance to experience her intimately. It also hinders the natural feel of that woman once they do experience her. They don't want her to hold back... They wanna feel all wetness, reaction, tightness... they want to bring her to orgasm, they want to feel love, without loving."

Ashlon nodded her head. The answers he gave her made her

understand her past better, and she needed to learn her past to cultivate the garden for her future.

"What do you love about me Devin?"

Devin grabbed her hand and kissed the back of it. He smiled at her. "I love the texture of your skin... from the beginning of your forehead to the end of your feet. I love the 10,000 watt light bulbs that you have for eyes, and the pillow stuffing that you have under your soft hands. I love the shape of your lips and the smoothness of your voice. I love the intelligence of your conversation, and the patience that you speak with. I love the way you respect me... You don't argue with me, you don't fight with me, you don't punish me for my past or for your past either. I love that I can be me around you... That I can love you without worry and without limits. I can go on and on, but just know that I'd talk your ears off literally in answering that question. All in all, you're my wife, my soul-mate, my best friend, my rider and I'm your equal. I don't see you as inferior or incompetent. I don't see you as an obligation or a bitch. I don't see you as a short term partner or a sexual conclusion... I see you as my life's heartbeat, and I pray daily that I can grow to be good enough so that you feel the same about me as I do you."

Devin's way with words always left Ashlon speechless. It was something that had been happening ever since the first time she saw him in the studio in action. His words came out perfectly crisp then, and came out the same way regardless of the time lapse. She was so happy with him and when she thought back to how her life was without him, she cringed and pulled him closer to her.

"Ashlon I wanted to talk to you about some stuff..." Devin said as his tone lowered.

"What's wrong baby?" Ashlon sat up, detecting sadness in his voice. "Talk to me, what's the matter?"

Devin exhaled. "Well... it's about business."

"What's wrong? It's going great Devin I'm proud of you."

"Well... Yea it's going great now, but I'm not rapping about the subjects that made me popular, and my core fanbase isn't going to support the new me the way they supported the rock star version of me."

Ashlon shook her head. "Why would you say that baby? You've just had the most successful album release in the last 4 years. #1 records, and sold out shows; your guest verses are selling at a premium, and you've been offered so many product placement deals, how could you think that your fans won't support you?"

Devin nodded his head. "Yea, I know what my record label reports, but they inflate some of the details for a public showing. You know they have their reputation on the lines as well. The public may see one version from the record label, but I have a realistic version and view whenever I go to the bank. Also, my last show... it wasn't as sold out as they reported it to be. My last few tour dates have been gradually losing interest and ticket sales."

"Well my investment firm is going great Devin, so it doesn't matter what happens, we're always going to be good. Don't worry about that. You've done everything a man is supposed to. You've taken care of your family on the highest of levels, and I want you to know that you didn't invest into no dummy. I got you baby."

Devin sighed as he stared at her. "I love that about you... but you know I wanna be able to always provide. I'm a man and that's my job."

"Baby— How about you just... Just get back in the studio and give them another hot project. You remember when DMX did that a long time ago? He dropped two albums in the same year when he was at his peak with Ruff Ryders. I think—"

"I don't really want that Ashlon. Honestly... I'd rather raise my daughters and work on signing and developing new artists. It's really not safe these days in the music industry with so many kids coming out of the streets and not fully understanding life. These kids are beyond reckless, and the major record labels are using their recklessness as a marketing strategy. It's just different."

"Baby you can still raise the girls while continuing on with your music. You know Ayeeka looks up to you? You're the only male role model she's ever had in her life. My little girl absolutely adores you, and I can see that you feel the same way about her. Whenever we're alone, you're all she talks about. She recites the radio version of your songs, and she's been writing music as well. She says she wants to be a singer like you when she grows up. Your daughter and my daughter adore each other, and they call themselves going to surprise you with a singing group for your birthday. Don't tell them I said it." Ashlon laughed as she thought about their little group.

"A singing group?" Devin laughed as he shook his head.

"Yes! A singing group!" Ashlon laughed along with her husband. "Ayeeka doesn't know the first thing about singing, but you've inspired her so... Just take her to the studio with you the next time you go and it's going to make her so happy. Devin I thank you for the way you treat my daughter."

"Our daughter." Devin said quietly.

Ashlon wiped a tear from her right eye and lay back against his chest. It was moments like those that shut her down with contentment for the night. She fell asleep praying for God to keep them safe, and for God to keep His angels camped around their household.

Devin's phone rang shortly after his wife fell asleep, and he muted it so that it didn't disturb her. When he saw his daughter's name on the caller ID, he slid from under Ashlon so he could go talk without disturbing her. He walked into the hall and answered.

"Hey baby."

"Daddy I wanna' live with you." Angel cried into the phone.

"Baby why are you crying?" Devin walked briskly back into the room and slipped his shoes on and grabbed his keys. He was getting dressed, and his movements and voice was waking Ashlon up, but he was seeing red at the moment.

"I just don't wanna be here anymore Daddy."

"Did somebody touch you?" Devin yelled. "Did somebody hurt you?"

"No Daddy! I just don't wanna live here! I wanna live with you and Ashlon."

"Alright baby I'm on the way to come get you right now!"

"Thank you Daddy."

He hung up and glanced at the time. It was after midnight and his daughter was calling him crying to leave her mother's house. He didn't like that one bit, and he was going to make sure to get to the bottom of the situation once he made it over there.

"What's wrong with Angel baby?" Ashlon asked as she climbed up in the bed and took her covers off.

"Nothing baby. Get your rest."

"No tell me what's wrong. Devin what's going on?"

"Nothing baby." He put his shirt on and fastened his belt.

"She wants to live with me and you. She wants me to come get her, she was crying."

Ashlon jumped up and put her shoes on.

"Ashlon where are you going?"

"With you. We gotta go get her."

Devin shook his head. "No, you stay here with Ayeeka, I'll be right back."

"Devin, Ayeeka can go with us. This is a family affair. It's no issue, I wanna go and see what's going on too."

"No... I need you to stay here Ashlon. Just let me handle this. Please."

Ashlon reluctantly sat back down on the bed. Her heart was beating a thousand times a second, but no matter how much she wanted to go along with her husband, she decided to stay being obedient to his word. It was killing her to do as he told her, but instead of arguing with him, she gave him the peace he needed in order to make the sound decisions that needed to be made throughout the night. She watched him walk out and dropped down to her knees in prayer. It was the one thing that she could do to always be in control of every situation. It was the one thing that would ensure that she was never left out when assistance was needed. It was the one thing that was more powerful than anything she'd ever seen on God's green earth. The power of prayer.

Devin wasted no time getting in his Bentley truck and making it to his baby mother's house. He would do anything for his daughter regardless of what time of day or night it was. He wasn't a fan of pulling up anywhere unannounced, but hearing the emotion in his daughter's voice did something to his spirit. He knocked on the door with the force and authority of a police officer. His patience was shot, so it wasn't long after the first series of knocks that he was back knocking on the door again. He was taking weight off of his left foot and redistributing it to his right foot, and alternating between right back to left; unable to stand still.

Brown answered the door bare-chested, rocking a pair of basketball shorts. "Devin."

"Send my daughter out here." Devin wasn't interested in any conversation.

"What's up Q Money Mack? How you been stranger?"

"Send my daughter out here." Devin repeated, looking into Brown's eyes with his own cold piercing set.

"Damn... No conversation for an old friend?"

Devin stared at him. "Boy I'ma give you to the count of 3—"

"Baby who's at the door?" Lika said as she walked from around the corner and stood next to Devin's old friend. Brown put his arm around Lika and smiled at Devin. "Oh hey... What brings you here at this time of night?" Lika glanced at the time.

"Send my daughter out here." Devin said for the final time. He was getting pissed at the both of them for the charade they were putting on.

"Well Devin I'm sorry... I'm not sending her anywhere because she still hasn't finished her chores. She has to wash the dishes and clean up the kitchen before she leaves this household. We have rules."

"Mommy I didn't even eat!" Angel said as she overheard their conversation while coming out of her room.

"I don't give a fuck if you ate or not. You had the option to eat and you didn't. Go clean the kitchen." Lika said with her hand on her hip.

"Angel come out of this house. Now!" Devin yelled through the house.

"Aye man calm your voice. You gon wake the baby up." Brown said while taking his arm from around Lika.

"Nigga shut the fuck up talking to me. I'ma give y'all one chance to let my daughter out of this house or I'ma fuck shit up for everybody in this house. This ain't the type of games you wanna play nigga. I swear to God you don't wanna play these games with me. I already let you live when you're supposed to die for the shit you've done. Don't get killed playing with me nigga. And Lika, you know how I get down so you better fuckin stop playing with me too."

Lika rolled her eyes and pulled her man by the hand. "Come on baby, let's go to bed. Angel go ahead and go to your daddy's *mansion*. Have fun and don't come back until you're ready to do those chores."

Brown stared at Devin and nodded his head with a menacing look on his face. He stepped back and let Angel out of the house with her suitcase in her hand. Devin picked her suitcase up and grabbed her hand. He was prepared to die for his daughter and his wife. He would do anything for his family, and would never be in the mood to play about anything that he loved. He turned and walked away.

"Devin you know how I play too nigga." Brown said to his back. "I don't think this is what you want at all."

Devin continued to walk while ignoring Brown's comments. He wasn't about to address adult business in front of his child, but he made a mental note to make sure he addressed him for tryna play like he was a tough guy. He knew that Brown was only trying to impress Lika, but he wasn't going to let that shit slide. He was going to teach him a lesson about trying to disrespect him in front of his daughter.

"Put your seatbelt on." He told Angel once they were inside the Bentley truck.

"O.K. Daddy."

"Hey listen... Let me make this clear to you Angel... You don't have to go back in that house at all ok? You can stay with me and Ashlon as long as you want if you want to. You can stay forever as far as I'm concerned. You don't ever have to be in a situation where you're not comfortable. I love you and I'm going to make sure that you're happy."

"O.K. Daddy. Thank you."

He turned the music on to a blank instrumental so he could start piecing songs together in his head. He had a million things on his mind and knew he needed to hit the studio first thing in the morning to express his feelings. He didn't even notice his daughter moving her lips and nodding her head until he was pulling into the neighborhood that he lived in.

"Are you rapping Angel?"

Angel looked at him nervously and looked away shyly. "No sir." She said with fear in her voice.

"It's ok Angel. If you're rapping you're rapping. I don't mind if you rap... What were you saying, and why do you have that look on your face?"

"It's just that... Brown gets mad when I rap and my Mama told me not to rap ever again."

"Well I'm not your mama and I'm sure as hell not Brown. You can rap around me all you want. I just wanna hear what you were saying." Devin said as he pulled into the circular white stone driveway.

"I said... The only thing I really want is my Daddy, I just wanna be a princess and be happy." Angel blushed and looked away nervously. "I know it's not good but I just—"

"Baby that's amazing! I love it. You sound better than I sounded when I first started rapping. Keep it up ok?"

Angel looked at her father wide-eyed. "You really think I'm good?"

"I think you're amazing. You're going to be one of the best rappers ever one day, but don't rush it baby. Just remain a princess for as long as you can. It's many princesses who became Queens too quick and they wish they could pick up a smaller crown for just one day. Enjoy these one days, one by one."

"Yes Father."

BLACK BARBEE

The club atmosphere was intense and electric. Despite marijuana still being illegal in the state of Georgia, every person in the club was blowing smoke like a chimney in the middle of winter. The pressure from the bass of the speakers was loud enough to rattle the process of logical thought, and the constant flow of alcohol mixed with the ever powerful presence of drug culture set the stage for many future regrets. The VIP sections had the who's who of Atlanta– the top dope boys, the most known gang members, a few players from the Atlanta Hawks, a few football and hockey players, rappers, singers, producers and actors.

Atlanta was a city that prided itself on image and presentation, and the more dazzle and shimmer you could present to the world of Atl; the more important you were to the world of Atl. You can't be someone of importance if you went to a club in Atlanta without being in a VIP section– this was the mentality of the streets, and it was the absolute only reason that people spent $4,000 on sections in the middle of the week, and came back and did it again for the weekend.

Showmanship. There were four levels of men in the showmanship capital– Men who drove Bentleys, Lamborghinis, and Rolls

Royces ran the city. Men who drove *used* Bentleys, and Lamborghinis, and Rolls Royces *appeared* to run the city. Those men got the same benefits as the men who ran the city, but their personal lives were usually in shambles. The 3rd level of men were those who drove Mercedes, Maseratis, Hellcats and Lexuses– regardless of if they were new or old; they just fit in as men who were still trying to come up. Then you had the guys driving the normal cars– these were the ones who were trying to do the right thing and were trying to be honorable men to their two or three women.

This mentality only applied to those who ran the streets, not the working class man or the married man.

Black Barbee had been born and raised in Atlanta, so she knew all too well about the city's culture and habits, so at all of her shows she made sure to always be kind to the niggaz who spent all of the money in the VIP sections to keep them supporting her. She only started rapping because of the popularity of her "So Gone" challenge when she posted it on Facebook. She had been going through a bad relationship, and only did the freestyle as a way to express herself. The challenge quickly went viral, getting her nearly 20 million views in less than a month, and it had been a gift and a curse.

When she walked backstage to do her pre-show preparation, she had a thousand emotions and two thousand thoughts running through her body. She was excited that the city had come out to support her, while simultaneously being angry that her boyfriend would try her like that. Her heart was beating so hard that she could hear the thump of it against her chest. She closed her eyes and pulled her phone out. No way could she let him get away with what he'd done.

"Hello?" He picked up on the first ring.

"You called the cops on me?"

"Black... Listen... Where have you been stashing your money at?"

Black Barbee frowned. She couldn't believe her ears. "What are you talking about?"

"Where you leave the money at?"

"So... you think—"

"I don't got time to talk bitch. Where is the money? Either you're gon tell me where it is or you better not come back to this house bitch. I'm not letting you in. You can go sleep at the fuckin shelter like you were before you moved in with me."

"This is about money? That's why I never told you about how much I was making because I knew you would do this shit. I just—"

"Bitch you been holding back! I've been buying all the shit we've been smoking and you been keeping a fucking secret! I thought we were in this shit together! Now I see that it was just you keeping it all for you!"

Even though she was angry at her boyfriend for calling the police on her, a part of her felt bad for holding out on him. She sighed. "I don't have anything saved up... But the more shows I get, the more money I can make. I was trying to work to get us a place—"

"Ain't no us." He barked, pissed. "It's just me, then it's just you. You don't need to get *us* shit. Bitch you go your way and I go mine. I can't fuck with no bitch who keep secrets. You out here getting money and I'm out here looking like a fool, doing stupid shit to keep us shit to smoke, meanwhile you just letting me do the shit."

"That's not true! I've given you some money after every show! Are you so high that you can't even remember that it was me paying for 90% of the shit we smoke? What's with you?" And as she said it, she heard the error of the moment in her own words. She closed her eyes and thought about how much crack they'd bought the last time they went out, and she knew that they didn't even use 25% of it. That's why he had given her the shit to take with her, because he had so much left. He'd tried to play her and it was burning her up inside.

"You're high." She said with regret in her voice. "You're fuckin high."

"Fuck you! Fuck you bitch! I don't fuckin' need you. Don't bother coming back to this house. Period."

"But... Where am I going to go? I've been helping you with everything since the first day we met... I don't understand why–"

The cold truth of the dial tone was enough to burn her up inside. She didn't understand why the world had to be such a cold place when all she wanted to do was live and be happy. She squeezed the phone as tight as she could and closed her eyes to try to calm down before hitting the stage. She didn't have long however, as the DJ was calling her name and the crowd was already going crazy anticipating her presence. The promoter walked up to her with a huge grin on his face. He handed her another envelope and shook his head.

"Thanks to you... we made five times more than we estimated we were going to make. I felt it was only fair to give you an extra $3,000 for blessing us with your presence. We appreciate you at this club. Thank you."

She grabbed the envelope, folded it and tried to stuff it in the pocket of her jeans. She took a deep breath and walked out to the stage amidst applause and whistles. She grabbed the microphone and said a quick silent prayer. She always performed the same few songs off of her mixtape, but she also did a unique freestyle at the beginning of each show depending on what she was going through at the time.

"Thank you all for coming out here and supporting me... I appreciate you all."

The strippers even stopped dancing while staring at Black Barbee's beautiful and enchanting presence. She was truly gorgeous– baby soft skin, soft brown eyes, soft natural hair, plump natural lips, perfect shape... She was everything a woman could dream of, however; nobody knew her secrets. From the outside, she was one of the most beautiful women in Atlanta, but on the inside she was dying inside mentally while struggling with spiritual depression.

I'm on so many drugs they all fuckin with each other/
The coke fucks the weed, the alcohol makes them cuddle/
The Percs make them nut, the wine pulls off the rubber/

It's crazy everything find love while I suffer-
Niggaz steady crossing me, drag me through the gutta/
My last nigga really thinking fuck me while he fuck me/
Stealing from me while I'm giving to you like it's nothing/
Leave me down and out I'm asking God why I'm unlucky-
Thirsty for a real nigga, I need one to build with me/
One to count a mil with me, fuck a bad bitch with me/
Where the real niggas? The ones'll keep it real with me/
The one that won't embarrass me I hope you feel me-

    OG stood stunned as he listened to Black Barbee's performance. She was more amazing than he'd expected her to be. Even if his son hadn't told him to come recruit her, she would be someone he'd want to get to know on a personal level. Despite her being younger than him, he couldn't deny the stunning level of attraction he was feeling for her. She had an old soul about her, a hurt vibe, one that made her feel approachable even if she was indeed out of his league. He shook his head and took a deep breath. He had to make sure to keep it business because he didn't wanna let his son down; but the desire...

    He watched her for the remainder of the show and was about to leave the VIP area to try to catch her before she left the strip club, but sat back down when he saw her walking to the VIP area. She was stopping at every table and person in the VIP taking pictures and shaking hands. All of the women were anxious to hug her, and all of the men were anxious to shoot their shot. The way she worked the room was amazing. It was almost as if she'd done it before in another lifetime. She had star power written all over her.

    The further she made it to where he was sitting, the more nervous he was getting. He knew what he was supposed to be doing, but for some reason his heart and mind was telling him something completely different. He had to get it together to represent for his son's record label. There was no way he was going to embarrass Q Money Mack while lusting over his assignment.

    "Black Barbee. Hey, I'm OG Terrance from–"

"Oh shit! Mack Money Records? It's such a pleasure!" Black Barbee said as she fanned her face as if she was about to cry.

Her humbleness put OG at ease, as he was expecting her to be as arrogant and conceited as she looked. He reached his hand out to shake hers and it amazed him at how excited she was about the handshake. He could sense the nervous vibe, and it made him handle her more delicately than he normally would.

"I'm sure many record labels have already approached you?" OG asked as he stared at the beautiful woman. She was even more mesmerizing up close and personal.

"Actually no... Nobody's approached me at all." She said while staring wide-eyed.

"Wow, that's incredible. As talented as you are... Well that's their loss. Would you be interested in signing with Mack Money Records? Q Mack had me come out personally to extend you an offer to sign with us."

Black Barbee looked as if she was going to faint. Tears ran down her face and she raised up and down on her tips toes while staring at OG in amazement. "Please don't be joking with me." She cried. "I've been let down so many times... I've been hurt so much... Please don't hurt me... Please be for real... Please don't just be telling me this for nothing... God please don't let him be playing with me."

Listening to the passion in her voice let OG know that she had great future ahead of her. She was one of the humblest women he'd ever been in the presence of, and she had every right to be as arrogant as she wanted to be but choose not to spew that into the world. "Listen... give me your number, I'll give you mine, and we can touch base in the morning. I'll let Q Mack know that you're interested in signing, and possibly set a meeting between you two up if you're free tomorrow."

The look on Black Barbee's face told the story of her life. He'd been around long enough to recognize hurt and disappointment whenever he saw it. He could see that she'd been abused by the cycle of life, and prayed that him and Q Mack could help her pull out of the cycle she'd been going through. He was excited that he'd succeeded in doing what his son asked him to do, and even more excited about getting to know Black Barbee. He knew she would probably want a younger, better looking, or more popular man; and he wasn't even mad. She was so spell-binding of a woman that he felt good just to get a chance to work with her in any capacity. She put her number in his phone, and he text her phone so that she could have his phone number as well.

"You be safe tonight... I'll call you first thing after making arrangements with Q Mack. Thank you for being so... humble... and beautiful..."

Black Barbee looked at him carefully. For a moment she thought she saw a spark in his eye, but chalked it off to her being excited. She blushed on a delayed reaction when she thought about his words. "Thank you..." She said slowly and smiled. She was so excited to be getting an opportunity to show her talent to the world that she didn't know how she was going to sleep that night.

"Thank you so much for the opportunity." She said as she clasped her hand together as if she was about to go into prayer.

A group of strippers walked up to her smiling and asking for hugs and pictures. OG smiled and turned away to let her handle her business for the night. He knew his son could turn her into one of the biggest superstars ever, and for a minute wondered if he would feel the same urges about her as he did. After all, his son had eyes, urges, and emotions just like any other man. Although he was happily married...

He quickly brushed those thoughts out of his head and prayed that his son did the same. He left out of the club and climbed into his 2018 Maybach. It was a car that was bought to him as a gift by his son and his daughter-in-law. When he thought about how powerful of a couple they were, he realized how foolish and childish his thoughts seemed. OG had spent so many years behind bars that he constantly caught himself walking a fine line between the principles of manhood and the principles of being just another nigga.

Instead of him being a role model for his son, it had swiveled to be the other way around. He was constantly learning from him and trying to grow as a man. He knew he had a long way to go, and thanked God for even giving him the opportunity to grow. He pulled off in his Maybach and headed to his Buckhead sky rise penthouse. When he was in prison he couldn't have imagined that he was going to be pushing a car that cost $160,000 while living in an apartment that cost $8,000 a month. An *apartment*. Life had truly taken a turn for the better, and he had his son to thank for it all.

DEVIN

The new Forbes magazine had been released and it was pissing him off. They had him listed as the top grossing Hip Hop act, meanwhile his bank account didn't reflect the information that his parent record label was releasing to the press. He understood the need to put him in a positive light, but he felt they were going a little bit too far with the exaggerations. He picked up his cell phone and went and sat in his Bentley truck to place a call to Ben Bland, his personal account manager.

"Hi Q Money!" Ben said with joy in his voice. "Did you see what we did for you?" He was saying it like they'd done him a favor.

"Why the fuck do y'all keep doing this shit? You're not doing anything to increase my finances, but y'all keep on exaggerating these numbers and making shit harder for me. Do you know what they're trying to charge me to do my fuckin grass these days? Five hundred fucking dollars. Do you know what they want for an instrumental for me to record music on? Fifty thousand dollars a beat. I can't get any type of discount on shit you know why? Because y'all keep lying about this fuckin money I'm making. Stop putting that shit out man! Help me make money instead of helping yourself to every dollar I make. That's' just dumb."

"I understand Q Money." Ben said in the same tone that he had when he first answered the phone. It was as if he was in his own world and not paying attention to the problems that Devin was presenting to him.

"Do you really understand though? Because at this rate I'm going to be fuckin broke because my record label wants to do more flexing and lying than these fuckin rappers. Speaking of which... Do I have any royalties coming? I haven't gotten any royalties in quite a while, and Billboard is reporting 8 million records sold."

"We paid you an advance remember?" Ben said, his voice still jubilant, unwavering in his excitement. He was like an emotionless robot.

"You paid me $2 million a year ago... You reported to Forbes that I brought in $80 million. I haven't seen anything other than the $2 million. That's not right. If you're exaggerating to Forbes, at least send me a bonus or something. You telling me I don't have anything coming?"

Ben sighed. "See... that's not how it works. You signed your rights over in exchange for an advance."

"Yea, but I've obviously paid you the advance back several times. I'm just asking if I have some type of bonus or anything else coming to me. I've been trying to make it by saving and being reasonable, but meanwhile y'all putting more pressure on my life and not helping me take any pressure off of me."

"Well I understand your frustration." Ben said while seeming to think about his next statement. "It is almost time for you to renew your contract with us, so how about we offer you $7 million up front this time around."

"And royalties?"

"No royalties. The same contract you signed last time remember?"

Devin sighed. He really needed the contract the last time because he was trying to get back on his feet. When he looked at the whole picture, he realized that he was in the same boat again, and the more he kept repeating the cycle, the more he would always be in the same predicament. It was a nasty cycle of repeating advances and contracts– a system created in order to create dependence on the artist so that they'll never have what they desire, and only what they need. From the outside looking it, it seemed as if the artists were living a dream life. Devin had gone down that cycle in the past and wasn't too fond of how it played out the first time around.

"Give me time to think about it." He said as he sighed while thinking about his constant flow of bills. He really wasn't in a position to take the deal, nor was he in a position to not take it. He truly did need time to talk it over with the ones who cared about him and understood his predicament.

"Take your time Q Money! Give me a call when you're ready! I'll be waiting!"

Ben was so arrogant that it made Devin sick to his stomach. He turned the phone off without replying, and pulled up his text messages to let the engineer know to meet him at the studio, but before he could press send his phone rung. He looked at the name on the caller ID, and instantly got excited. If his Dad was calling him that early in the morning, then that must have meant good news for everyone.

"Hello?"

"Hey son. I have good news for sure..."

"Aight lay it on me." Devin had a huge smile on his face. That was going to be the one signing that fixed his finances forever. She was a brilliant artist, and he was going to take her to the top of the industry. He wasn't rapping about the same stuff since his life was different, and she was literally the rock star of the modern era that he was of yesteryear. It was a perfect artist acquisition, because he would also be showing her how to handle the spotlight the way he didn't have anyone to teach him.

"First of all, I wanna say to you that God is amazing."

"Yes He is. That will forever be true. What's up Pops?"

OG started laughing out of excitement. He calmed down a notch to not appear over anxious. "Well... I met Black Barbee last night. I first wanna tell you... I think she's an amazing woman period. She's as humble as any woman I've ever met, and she was so excited about having the opportunity to sign to Mack Money Records. I told her I would arrange a meeting between you two today. She was all for it. So what time do you wanna arrange this meeting? Devin let me tell you... This woman is so gorgeous in real life that it's really insane."

Devin thought about it for a minute and nodded his head. It was as if his older self was speaking to his younger self. "Pops you handle it. The offer to her is a $250,000 signing bonus plus 40% of her royalties. Stop by my lawyer's office and get the paperwork together for her. I trust you to manage her Pops. I'll meet her when or if necessary, but for the most part, you're in charge of her. You're her manager, and you're responsible to get the most out of that particular artist. I don't need to disrespect my wife by smiling in that woman's face when I already know my weaknesses."

OG Terrance learned so much about life by listening to his son talk. It was another learning experience for him that morning, and he was going to apply it to his thought process going forward.

Never be too willing to expose yourself to your weaknesses. Find ways to curve your weaknesses by forming buffers between your vices and your heart. Putting others in positions of importance puts the burden of execution in such a way that the people elected to carry out these orders raise the bar in order to live up to the level of trust.

He knew that his son trusted him to do the right thing, and he fully planned to make him proud. "I got you son. You know that."

"Appreciate that Pops. You know I don't trust many. You and my wife is what it boils down to. I need you to get her signature on that contract and get her into the studio. Get her working. I want 100 songs recorded in the next 3 weeks. Start building her work ethic up so that it becomes natural to her."

"I got you son."

"Aight cool. I'm about to hit the studio myself, so I'll touch base with you later."

"Aight later."

Devin rolled the Forbes magazine into the shape of a cone and walked back in the house. He went to the living room and grabbed his backpack off of the coat hanger, then walked in the kitchen and tossed the magazine into the trash. He walked into the bedroom and kissed his wife.

"Baby... I'm headed to the studio. I have some work to do."

Ashlon was sitting in the bed on her computer reading over some potential investments for her clients. She had 7 spreadsheets laid in front of her on the bed, and it was a cup of coffee on the nightstand. She put a single finger to her lip motioning for Devin to quiet down. Noticing the confused look on her face, she pointed right beside her. His heart warmed when he saw Angel and Ayeeka both laying side by side sleeping in the spot he normally slept in.

"They came and got in the bed not too long after you went out the house." She whispered.

"They're so spoiled." Devin tried to whisper, but the joy in his voice pulled the volume of his whisper loud enough to wake Ayeeka up.

"Good morning!" Ayeeka said while stretching. She shook Angle gently. "Wake up Angel it's morning again."

Angel opened her eyes and looked at her father's backpack. "Daddy I wanna go to the studio with you."

"Me too." Ayeeka said with a big grin on her face.

It was no way he could possible reject their requests. They had him wrapped around his finger, and they knew it. He was the weakest person in the world when speaking to them and honoring their requests, and the strongest person in the world when protecting them.

"Your father has work to do girls. Don't y'all wanna go get your nails done today?" Ashlon asked while trying to take the pressure off of her husband.

Devin quickly interjected. "Actually... they can come with me, and I'll take them to the nail shop when I go get a haircut since it's right next door."

"You sure Devin?" Ashlon laughed while trying to picture him walking into the nail shop with two young bosschicks. "Do you know what to ask for?"

"Yea... acryllya?"

"You mean acrylic right?" Ashlon and the girls started laughing.

"I want metallic gel." Angel said with all of her teeth showing. She was much happier spending time with her father and her stepmother than she was spending time with her mother and stepfather. It was nothing but pure happiness and love in her father's home.

"I want metallic gel too!" Ayeeka said grinning.

It was amazing the bond that Ayeeka and Angel shared with each other.

"Alright. Metallic gel for everyone. Girls go ahead and get dressed so we can handle everything." Devin said with a soft smile on his face. He was amazed at how his life had gone from one extreme of depression to another extreme of being a family man in a year's time. He always pictured his life being that way, but deep down inside it was only a fantasy of his; it wasn't reality.

"Baby..." Devin started as he sat on the bed beside his wife. "The new Forbes magazine came out today listing the Hip Hop Power Earners."

"Oh great! You're number one right?" She said with a sheepish grin on her face.

"So you already know?"

"Of course I know Devin. It's the first thing I saw when I logged onto social media this morning. Congratulations baby."

"They're exaggerating the numbers Ashlon. I didn't make that much, not even close..."

Ashlon wrapped her arm and leg around Devin and kissed him on the back. "Baby... stop worrying... We're going to be fine. I know you always tell me to stop worrying about keeping us together, and I want you to stop worrying about finances. We're going to be perfectly fine. My business is going great, and yours is also. True it may be a slight exaggeration, but baby we're good. We got each other."

Ashlon's words were comforting and much needed. He sat on the edge of the bed soaking in the touch of his wife's hand, the magnetic feel of the gold on her wedding band rubbing across his back– the warmth of her breath against his back, the soft fragrance of her hair, the luxurious elements of completion soaking into his being. He was happier than he'd ever been in his entire life, and he had her to thank for it. God had truly showered His greatest blessings on his household, and he was so thankful.

"Let's go to church on Sunday."

Ashlon smiled at her husband's words. She loved the changes that she was seeing in him, and was thankful for the continuous effort he'd been showing. Effort showed that he wanted the relationship just as bad as she wanted it. Effort reminded a woman that she was not alone, and provided her with the fuel needed in order to match her man's strength. A woman couldn't match a man who couldn't show her what to match.

"Yes baby. I can't wait."

Devin turned and kissed her. The passionate fire from kiss number 2,793 was the same glow that bestowed on them from kiss #1. It was the most accurate definition of love. The level of love that brought tears out of the eyes of a witness, fear out of the heart of the devil, and blessings from the presence of the Lord.

It was the kind of love that authors stayed up all night trying to write about, producers spent thousands of hours out of their lives trying to make movies about, and the kind that singers stayed in the studio for hours at a time in order to relay the emotion to someone who's never felt it before. It was greater than riches, and more valuable than 3 wishes. It was rare and unique– refreshing in a modern era where love was temporary and based on what you could do for another person. It was old school love reborn and reissued.

"I love you Devin."

"I love you too Ashlon."

Devin squeezed her hand gently and got up to see if the girls were ready. They had a full day ahead of them, and he didn't want to delay it.

"We'll see you later baby."

"OK. I'll be in the bed finishing up my work. Drive safe."

BLACK BARBEE

The rooms in the Westin Hotel in downtown Atlanta provided some of the most beautiful views that a person could ask for. The 62nd floor hotel room contained floor to ceiling windows, with a panoramic view of everything from Interstate 85 to the lights of Hartsfield International Airport to the outline of Stone Mountain. The city lights flickered like an eternal forest fire, and the presence of Mercedes Benz stadium provided a visual soundtrack to the city immersed in elegance and status.

The aroma of the strawberry ocean candle held a tight grip on the room's vibe. The temperature was just right for Barbee, but the 95 degrees she had the heat on was enough to run any normal person out of the room forever. She was sweating as if she had just been running up and down a basketball court, although she was only sitting in one spot.

She thought about her performance from the previous night and how great it made her feel to get so much love in a city that contained so much hate. She replayed things that was said to her, replayed in her mind the moments that women approached her and told her they loved her; and felt a brief hurt knowing that all of the love she'd ever experienced came from the hearts of strangers. She thought about the record label offer from Mack Money Records, and sighed.

"Mama." Barbee whispered in a ragged voice.

She was sitting in a chair at a workstation in the corner of the room. There was a computer in front of you, but it was still folded shut. She stared straight ahead at the blank wall, but her mind and eyes showing her moments of sadness and hurt, depression and pain.

"Mama why?" Tears rolled down her face and her lips quivered. Her mouth opened slightly as if to take a deep breath, but nothing went into her body except the memory of disappointment.

"Everytime I look at you I see that fuckin no good daddy of yours. Get the fuck out my face."

Her mother continuously took the disappointment from her father out on her. The random beatings at the hands of her mother. The neglect, making her eat cereal out of dog bowl, not teaching her what was going on when she had her first period, and making her go to school with no pads or tampons– her having to ask her teacher to help her stop the bleeding... Her never having her hair done, her mother punching her in the face while she slept.

"Mammaaaaa why?" Barbee cried bubbles of pain as she thought about her painful past. Her mother always kept the heat on 95 degrees in her room, but kept it cool in the rest of the house. She'd been punished mentally and physically for so long that she knew it was only one way out.

She exhaled and grabbed the pipe that gave her so much life and happiness. The sexy smooth feel of it plus the memory of how the smoke tickled her brain until it curled over in joy and laughter was exciting to her. She lit the crack pipe and inhaled the soulful vapors of pressure. Each rock was different to her and caused a different effect. This one scared her, it was so strong that she knew she would have to save the rest for later.

Her eyes were opened three times the size of normal, but to her nothing seemed different. Her brain felt like the smoke went up there and sat down, the pressure pressing against her skull, and her nostrils opened up as if she'd just taken a whiff of bleach and ammonia. Her throat felt like she'd just rubbed a cough drop against the lining of her esophagus.

An invisible massage went through her body at a rapid pace, and it made her jump up in the air. Her movements were four times faster and she was clumsier than normal. She tried to stand and lost her footing, stumbled to catch herself and tripped up over a trash can. Sweat poured down her beautiful face, and between the sweat and the tears, it looked as if she'd just jumped out of a swimming pool.

Her heartbeat sped up quicker, but she was used to it. The powerful effects from the crack cocaine made it so that she could literally see her heart beating if she closed her eyes. She felt a pain... An unusual pain... She grabbed her chest with her left hand and stopped breathing in order to see if that would help the pain go away, but instead the pain started becoming worse.

She had a motto that she lived by... *I'm no stranger to pain, but I can be a pain to strangers.*

But she'd never experienced pain on the level that she was feeling it. She jumped up off of the floor and opened the door to her hotel room. She went left, and turned and went right; but with both directions looking the same, she didn't know where to go. She knocked on the door next to hers and screamed as she fell back and slammed against the wall. Her eyes shut. Her mind shut. The pain left.

OG TERRANCE

I'd spent so many years behind bars that I still found myself doing the things I would do if I was still locked up. I had to catch myself... Sometimes I would go hours without breaking my mindset away from the imprisonment of the white man's zoo. I woke up in the morning and when I realize that I'd slept with my boots off, I got nervous and afraid. I jumped up and put my boots on with the speed of a cheetah.

Men are ageless in prison. This means a 21-year-old will stab a 55-year-old just for disagreeing with him. Disagreements happened a lot because of the time period capsules. You have 40 year olds who went to prison at 20, and they still have the life experience and thought process of a 20-year-old. So when they disagree with another 40-year-old... who could be actually 20 mentally, they wanna kill each other literally.

I was no longer in prison physically, but mentally I was fucked up. I appreciated everything that my son had done for me with helping me get my life together, but getting my mind together was an entirely different task. Many days I woke up angry at the world for taking my freedom away, only to remember that I was free.

Many days I woke up pissed at the United States for making me do so much time for petty crimes, only to remember that it was the past and I've been rewarded for my pain.

But rewarded pain still existed.

On the surface I carried smiles and happiness, brightness and love— but underneath the thin wrap that was a face, I carried hatred and darkness— sadness and madness.

They stripped me of my manhood. Fatherhood. My life. They took my best days from me only because I was unable to afford a lawyer. It hurt, and my soul bled when I slept and my soul suffocated when I was awake. I was pissed and ready to kill somebody every day, but every day I had to remember that I'm not in the dungeon anymore. I was a street nigga earning seven figures a year, but unable to enjoy it because of the hurt that was engraved into my soul.

I was slowly getting familiar with the real world, but it wasn't easy. Each day I had the task of scouring social media in the morning, after lunch, and after dinner. I had to make sure that all was good with my son, and make sure that I got our attorneys to send cease and desist letters out to blogs reporting false stories in exchange for likes and attention. It wasn't a hard job; it was just so foreign to me. I caught myself arguing with a bunch of bitch ass niggas on the internet at least twice a week. I let the women talk, but I couldn't excuse the niggaz for acting like hoes. Fuck them niggaz.

I thought about Black Barbee and her alluring eyes... Her sensual voice... When I shook her hand, the softness of her palm made me have a wet dream about how soft the rest of her body could possibly be. I didn't know much about her, yet I felt like I could love her; flaws and all. Meeting a woman that beautiful yet that down to earth was a blessing. It wasn't something that happened every single day, but for some reason God had seen fit for it to happen to me. Then there was the age difference... but...

She was beyond amazing. She was so beautiful that it seemed

like a talent to look so good. Her followers on all of the social media sites all thought the same as I did. They loved her pictures, and complimented her every single time she posted. We were still years apart... light years...

There was still a darkness to her that I never saw in her pictures. There was a darkness that could only appeal to a nigga who fought darkness daily. I saw her darkness, her fight, her struggles and pain. I saw her light, but I could recognize that it was wrapped around her darkest moments and days. I too had a brightness wrapped around the same dark shine... She would never like me... We're light years apart.

After my son let me know how much money to offer Black Barbee, I went and ate lunch instead of blowing up her phone and coming off as thirsty. Even though I had yet to contact her that day, she was the number 1 thing on my mind, and it had been that way since I first laid eyes on her. My mind was racing thinking about the potential to be more than a friend to Black Barbee, but I knew I needed to calm down instead of setting myself up for disappointment.

My phone rang while I was taking a bite of my sandwich. I unbit it when I saw my son's name on the caller ID.

"Hey boss."

"Hey pops. What's good?"

"Ahhh, I'm cool. Just having an ol' tuna sandwich. How about you?"

"I'm good... The girls are getting their nails done right now, and then I'm headed to the studio for a session."

"Alright alright. You need me at the studio? You need me to do anything for you?" I never wanted him to think that I was ungrateful. I didn't know anything about the music industry before he started making me learn it. He could have gotten anybody to do the job I was doing, but he insisted that I do it. It was so simple, sometimes I wonder if he even needed anybody to do the work I was doing.

"Nah I don't need you at the studio... but I need you to check on Black Barbee. My wife text me and said she saw something on social media saying she had to be rushed to the hospital."

"What? What happened?" Panic took over me. I'd just met her, yet the connection was so deep that it was like I'd known her forever. Maybe it was just her pain I'd recognized... Either way, I was familiar with it.

"It was something about an overdose."

The phone became silent. I'm sure we were both reflecting on my son's battle with overcoming addiction. It was a difficult fight, but it was one that had been handled.

"I'm going to find out what's going on with her." I said as I wrapped the sandwich up to discard it.

"Dad listen... See if she wants to accept that offer. If she accepts it, I don't want you to leave her side unless you have no other choice. I want you to be around her as much as possible. Get her in a good living situation and keep her away from drugs as much as possible. I know you know... She needs a strong support system and she needs to know that somebody's in her corner. Dad I don't wanna tell you what to do with your life, but we have to save her if she allows us."

"I'm on it son. I... She..." I had to catch myself from saying things that hadn't yet earned the airwaves. It was a habit from talking on the phone from behind prison walls. I never had much to say, so I would have to speak things that hadn't happened yet in order to have conversation with the people on the outside. "I'm going to get on top of that as soon as I hang up the phone with you."

"Aight. Well let me know how it goes and I'll get the lawyer to handle the rest."

"Ok son. Have fun with those girls. Be safe. One."

The blogs were reporting that Black Barbee had been taken to Emory Emergency Room, so I didn't hesitate to make my way. I was determined to try to save her spiritually if the doctors could do their jobs physically. I knew the pain I saw in her eyes was real.

I knew the happiness was a cover up to a dark cloud. I could spot pain light years away because I saw it in the mirror every day, and I saw it on the faces of men for decades. She was much too beautiful and talented... She was valuable to the world, and I was going to make sure that she understood that.

DEVIN

Our day was priceless. Spending time with my daughters and getting to know them more had proved to be more exciting than a deadbeat could ever imagine. To be fair... it took patience and timing to arrive at that level of manhood, and I was happy that I was able to experience it. They'd gotten their nails done to their liking, and even recorded some adlibs behind one of my songs from my next project. I was excited that they were getting experience in the studio, but I wasn't excited about some of the stuff that had taken place in the studio unit next to mine.

"Oooooooh!" A group of young niggaz yelled out once I walked out of the studio session with my daughters.

"Y'all leave him alone, he got his kids with him." One guy yelled out.

"Yea have some respect." Another one spoke, but I couldn't ignore the sarcasm in his voice.

It was one thing to play with me in any form or fashion, and it was an entirely different thing to play with me in front of my family– let alone play with me in front of my kids. I stopped the girls in their tracks and turned to face the guys.

"Leave who alone?" I asked, anger rushing to my lips.

One of the young guys started laughing and snickering, pissing me off even more. "Fuck you old head. You better mind yo' fuckin business."

"You talking to me?" I was seeing red and ready to black out, but I had to chill once I saw the bulge of the pistol on the nigga's waist. I had to get my daughters to safety first.

"You fuckin right I'm talking to you old head."

I looked in his face and realized that it was one of the rappers who'd been building his fan base by talking reckless to other rappers. He was always on the blogs having drama and beef towards somebody. He was always taunting, always telling people nobody could fuck with him. I blacked out eternally, but I knew I couldn't just react right in front of my daughters.

"Aight... I'll see ya." I turned and grabbed my daughters by the hands and walked with them outside of the studio. I started walking towards my Bentley truck and cringed when I heard the young niggas behind me talking crazy. I was fastening Ayeeka into her carseat when her words broke my heart.

"Why are they being rude to you Daddy?"

I continued fastening her seatbelt and made sure Angel was fastened into the seatbelt. I walked around the truck and froze once I got behind the truck. I stared at the group of young niggaz. They were laughing and joking, pointing fingers and probing my happiness. They were talking to me as if I was a nobody, and all for the sake of getting attention and record sales. They had people recording their every word, most likely about to send it all to the ShadeRoom or TMZ. I hated the way the new generation was going about things. In my generation, it was customary to pay homage to our favorite artists, but the new generation earned their stripes by clowning the people they looked up to.

"Aye... I'm not the one to fuckin play with." I spoke calm yet in a stern voice. I meant what I said– I wasn't about to play with no lame ass kids, and I definitely wasn't about to let them play with me.

"Shit... What you gon do about it old head?"

"What you want me to do about it? I can get it in blood right now if I need to."

"Shit you ain't saying shit!" The nigga said as he pulled his pistol off of his waist. I knew he had a pistol, but I guess I was thinking that he would shoot me a fair one... I was thinking that I would be able to get a fight in before a pistol came out... But the pistol came out first... I wasn't in position to have a shoot out with my daughters in the truck. Bullets had no address or destination– they just flew in a wild manner until it could seek an object to park into. I would have to handle that situation by myself instead of risk getting my daughters hurt.

"Aye... You got it boss... You got it..." I said as I waved my hands up.

It was 5 young rappers outside, and two of them had their pistols up ready to kill me. I shook my head in disappointment. I couldn't believe the level of disregard they were having towards me. I'd done so much to pave the way for them to be successful rappers, yet they didn't give the first fuck about all that. Social media had become their lives– it was more important for them to try to degrade a legend instead of paying homage like we would have done back in our days.

"Yea I know we got it. Now get your ass in the truck and be a family man nigga."

The young rapper had gold and purple streaks in his hair. His name was Drum Killer, and he had a huge following because of his wild antics. I looked him in the eyes and knew that he would rather break his ankle instead of kill an ant. When I looked in his crew's eyes, I couldn't say the same thing. They looked as if they had nothing to live for, and therefore were living their lives for him. Anything he was unable to do, he was able to do; as long as he was able to continue providing for them. His success was their success, and his beef was theirs.

I got in the truck and put my seatbelt on. I didn't even notice my hand shaking until Angle asked me if I was ok. I took a deep breath and calmed my nerves down.

"I'm fine baby. It was just a misunderstanding back there, that's all."

As I drove around the corner, I saw Drum Killer raise his gun in the air and bust shots in the sky. The sound of every bullet made me twitch. They were so fucking careless playing that dumb ass street nigga role. Firing a gun while I was with my daughters? I was a raging bull behind the steering wheel– so angry, yet so helpless. I knew I was going to pay them back for what they'd done to me... But I had to let my nerves calm down first. I turned the music up in the truck and toggled through my list of possible ways of retaliation methods.

Pretty soon I was on the expressway, my focus no longer on Drum Killer and his crew, but now on making sure nobody on the expressway ran me off of the road while I had my babies with me. With me no longer drinking alcohol and doing pills, my anxiety was through the roof these days. As I drove I had a panic attack, and a visualization of someone side-swiping my truck and flipping us over. I had a panic attack visualizing my daughters being unconscious and shaking... unable to move, and the thought of losing her. I glanced back in the backseat and saw their innocent eyes staring at me.

I calmed down and took a deep breath. I hit the locks on the doors to make sure they didn't open the door and fall out by accident. Every driver that got beside me on the expressway made me nervous. I shifted into the slow lane to get away from the speeding drivers. It didn't take but one drunk driver to pass out and wreck my truck. A tear fell from my eye and I panicked while thinking of the potential for having an accident. The pace of my heart was faster than the pace of my truck.

"God please protect us." I whispered against the thump of the speakers. At least when I drank alcohol and took drugs I never worried about things that hadn't happened. When I was under the influence I only thought about the stuff that had happened, and it wasn't long before I forgot about that as well. At that moment I knew a drink was something that would relax me, but I knew I couldn't go back down that path again. I promised my wife a new me and I planned on sticking to that.

My body didn't relax until I was pulling back up to our place. I took a breath of comfort as I looked in the mirror and didn't see anyone trailing us. My mind thought back to Drum Killer and how he'd disrespected me in front of my daughters. For a quick instant it raised my blood pressure again, but I wasn't going to carry that anger into my household. Tomorrow was going to be a new day.

"Y'all like y'all nails?"

The girls plastered huge smiles on their faces. "Yes!" They both said in unison, holding their hands out and admiring the work of beauty.

"Thank you daddy!" Angel said, her words being echoed by Ayeeka.

I wasn't Ayeeka's biological father, but the connection I felt to her was just as strong as the one I felt to Angel. I would do anything to protect them, and do anything to make sure nobody hurt them. I would die for these little girls, kill for them if I had to. I would punish my own soul for eternity to protect theirs. A father's love was special; a black father's love was a blessing– I knew this because of how I felt about being able to experience my own father's love.

We walked into the house and they ran to their rooms to play some computer based game called Roblox. Every time they mentioned it I made a mental note to check it out to see what it was all about. Maybe if I liked it enough I would invest into the company for providing my daughters so much excitement each day.

My wife smiled at me as I walked to my room. I managed a fake smile back, but she wasn't going for it.

"Uh unh. What's wrong with you baby?" She grabbed my arm like a dude grabbed a chick's arm at the club.

"Oh man... Love I really don't wanna discuss it. I just really don't."

"That's not the rules we have in our home." She reminded me.

I knew that of course, but I really didn't wanna drag that negative energy off of the streets into our bedroom. Whenever I experienced negativity, which was often; I always tried my best to rid that energy off of my conscious before coming back home. However, the negativity that I'd just faced was a little deeper than normal because I had my kids with me when it took place.

"Baby... please..." I said, pleading with my wife to let it go. "I don't wanna relive it right at this moment by discussing it, but I promise to discuss it later ok?"

Ashlon twisted her lips for a brief moment, but she didn't press it. I really appreciated the fact that she listened to me. I needed that quality in my woman. Granted she could pressure me into discussing it, or force me to speak on it, but she knew that didn't help us out in the long run. We didn't keep score either– which means that if the moment comes where she doesn't wanna discuss something, she's not going to say or play the *"You remember when..."* game. I loved this woman with all of my soul, for reasons that it would take another husband who loves his wife to understand.

I walked into the bedroom and lay on the bed. My intentions were to take a quick nap and get up and eat dinner, but I was so tired from stress that I slept through the night.

ASHLON

Sometimes I wish I could protect my husband from the harsh realities of the world. I wish I could turn into an angel sometimes and cover him in more than prayer. I loved my black man, and I hated that he endured so much on so many days. If it wasn't one thing it was another- women constantly throwing themselves at my husband, niggaz throwing their negative energy at my husband, the vulchers and the home-wreckers, the government, the cops, the gossip blogs and distasteful bloggers. I hated that he had to fight so much each day just to come home, but I had trust in him dearly because I knew no matter what his fight entailed; that he would not give up on us.

A woman like me... I needed to feel secure that my flaws wouldn't push him away from us. I needed to feel this to feel safe as a wife, as a mother, and as helpmate. It was ok to be angry, it was ok to disagree, it was ok to be yourself and to be a human; but it was never going to be ok to quit on each other, and we never did. I prayed so much because I knew it was the only thing I could do in a world so vicious and unpredictable. I prayed that we stayed who we were, I never prayed for us to reach a "next level," or for any materials; I only asked God to keep what He'd already blessed us with.

I fixed our plates and sat at the dinner table with the girls. I put my husband's food in the microwave in case he woke up in the middle of the night hungry and wanted something to eat besides me. I thought about waking him up, but I knew how hard it was for him to go to sleep when he had a lot on his mind, so I didn't disturb that.

"Angel. Ayeeka. I really like those color nails y'all have."

"Thank you!" Angel said.

"Thank you Mommy." Ayeeka said. "I wanted my nails to be like yours."

I smiled at her as she started telling me about all of the colors she saw at the nail shop. I ate my chicken and listened as Angel joined in telling me about a lady at the nail salon who had earrings on each of her fingernails. I was amazed, but not surprised. People were doing the most these days in a world that competed for attention and validation. I laughed when Ayeeka commented on how ugly the earrings looked. That little girl had too much sense.

"Y'all make sure to eat your broccoli ok? It's good for you. It'll make you smarter and healthier."
"Okay." They said in unison.

"Where's Daddy?" Angel asked, looking at the empty chair.

"He's resting baby. He was really tired. Y'all wore him out today."

"We didn't mean to wear him out." Ayeeka said. "I just wanna be nice to him."

I smiled at her. "Baby I'm just kidding. He loves you all, and he knows you're nice to him, and that's why he's nice to you also."

"The man at the studio was mean to him."

"Yea he was really mean to my Daddy." Angel repeated after Ayeeka.

"What man? What did he do?" I put my fork down and it felt like I was in the matrix– my world slowed down and it was as if all of the words were hitting me in slow motion. I was angry that my girls had experienced this, and I could only imagine how angry my husband was. I was suddenly angry for even asking him to tell me what was wrong.

"One of the guys with different colors in his hair–"

"He had like unicorn hair mommy!" Ayeeka said.

"Yea!" Angel had put her fork down too. "He was being really mean and saying really mean things to Daddy. He was saying bad words, and I heard a gun sound too."

"Alright alright. I want you all to finish eating y'all food ok? Don't worry about anybody being mean ok? All we can do is pray to God for these mean people and pray that He come bless their hearts to make them better people. Just because you all see other people be mean, I don't want either of you to be mean to other people ok?"

They nodded their heads as they ate their broccoli. "When y'all finish eating your broccoli, I have ice cream for y'all."

"Yayyyy!" They were in unison a lot of things, but no happiness sounded as harmonized as the reward of them both getting ice cream. They were excited, but deep down I was pissed. I excused myself from the table and went to the bathroom. I locked the door and turned the water on in the sink. Tears fell from my face as I thought about my girls talking about a *gun sound* while at the studio. I knew the rapper they were talking about, because he was always in the blogs trying to pick on somebody and cause controversy as if he was the baddest man in the land. I always saw that, and I always prayed that him and my husband never crossed paths.

I knew it was inevitable because we all lived in the same city, but deep down I was hoping that the young guy would have respect to my husband since he was a veteran who had lived the street life already. Apparently that just wasn't the case. I prayed for the strength and direction to know how to handle it as a wife. I prayed that my husband woke up anew and that this too simply passed without anything coming of it.

DEVIN

I woke up refreshed. It was almost 10 AM and I was hungrier than ever. I had been so angry the previous night that I fell asleep without even eating dinner. My wife had cooked both dinner and breakfast by the time I woke up, and I had a choice over which one I wanted. She was at her workstation with her robe on by the time I got out of the bed.

"Good morning baby." I said, but she didn't hear me because she had her headphones on. I got out of the bed and kissed her on the neck, startling her for a moment. She jumped, turned and blushed, then pulled me in for a kiss. I was insecure that morning because I knew I had morning breath. I needed to get myself together.

I grabbed my phone off of the nightstand and powered it on as I walked off to the bathroom. By the time I closed the door and the Apple logo opened the gates to my phone, a flood of message notifications invaded my screen. Every morning was the worst moments of my anxiety because there was no telling what type of fuckin scandal or bullshit rumors I would have to wake up and fight. Flashbacks of my previous fights against the rumor mill made my heartbeat double time.

It would seem like I would be used to the rumors at this point, since I'd dealt with it for so many years- but I was still just a human being. I still got nervous and scared at times, still got depressed and angry when people talked about me, still got in my feelings when people critiqued me. I think it so aggravating because people talked about me who didn't even mean it. It was just something to do to pass their time, just something to entertain them for a brief moment.

When the notifications slowed down, I was able to enter Instagram. As soon as I opened the app, there my name was in huge print.

DRUM KILLER DISSES Q MONEY MACK IN A NEW DISS SONG.

"Fuck!" I whispered as I closed my eyes and shook my head. I didn't do no damn battle rapping, nor did I even care about rap the way the rest of the industry did. My only goal was to take care of my family by doing the only thing that had ever worked for me- music. I'd even changed the content of my music to reflect my new spiritual growth, yet hear I was being tested again. I turned the volume down so my wife couldn't hear it, and I pressed play.

I got a pistol for a punk ass bitch/
Check his paperwork, Q Money a snitch/
Got a pistol for you boy, we don't play that nigga/
100 round AK your whole family get it-

I had to pull the phone away from my ear and take a good look at it. I had to scroll to make sure he was serious with the shit he'd just said, or if he said it by accident. I had to double check to see if it wasn't another Q Money he was talking about... But it wasn't.

He had chosen to talk shit about me when I absolutely had no sense about a nigga threatening my family. I turned the phone off and placed it in my pocket. I felt a sense of calm dust itself over my conscious in the form of a soothing blanket.

I smiled. I knew we would always be tested while living on God's green earth, but I knew just like He knew that there were certain tests that I would always, absolutely fail without a doubt. My anxiety was subsiding and everything became clear to me. I wasn't going to make the mistakes I made the last time I got arrested, but I knew for a fact that that nigga was as good as dead. I needed him cooked in the next 24 hours.

I scrolled past a few more Instagram posts, and another headline caught my eye.

WIFE OF Q MONEY MACK ENTERS THE FORBES LIST AS ONE OF THE MOST PROFITABLE INVESTMENT START-UPS

That headline wasn't really surprising to me, because my wife worked extremely hard. I was only mad that they didn't have her on the Forbes list way sooner. I continued brushing my teeth while deciding how I was going to celebrate with her. Despite the minor issues I constantly encountered, I had to admit that I was truly a blessed man. I had the type of life any man would dream of, but I wasn't flawless. I was nowhere near perfect, and Drum Killer was going to find that out later.

OG TERRANCE

I'd been sitting beside Black Barbee's hospital bed for hours as she slept. She was conscious, the nurse said; but her body had been tired, so her catching up on much needed sleep was very necessary for her recovery. Before coming here, I'd stopped at Wal-Mart and bought a dozen roses and some chocolates for her that I figured would brighten her day. I'd been locked up so long that I didn't even realize that people bought roses from Wal-Mart. They didn't even sell them back in my day. They'd become so advanced and efficient.

I'd been watching Sports Center all evening, night, and morning until a baseball game came on around 2 in the afternoon. I didn't even realize that I'd been sitting there for so long because I was used to sitting in a room with nothing happening. It was something that wasn't even a thought. I was so scarred from the experience of prison that it was unbelievable sometimes. After a while I got thirsty, so I left the flowers and chocolates on the table beside her and walked out to find a soda machine.

I saw the nurse in the hallway and stopped her.

"Excuse me ma'am. I'm looking for a soda machine. I'm kinda thirsty."

She smiled and nodded her head. "You should be. You've been sitting in the same spot for almost 24 hours straight."

I didn't even realize it had been that long. It didn't seem like that long, especially being in the presence of Black Barbee and admiring the beauty that her face held. She literally looked like a living doll to me.

"I wish my father loved me the way you love your daughter." The nurse said. Her words broke my heart, but I didn't show it; at least I tried not to show my hurt by smiling at her.

"There is a gift shop down on the 2nd floor. There are beverages and items there to eat. Your daughter should be awake shortly, so you may want to grab her something as well."

I turned and walked away without saying thank you. It was like she'd stabbed me with a knife, took it out and put it back in the same hole. I guess it made sense though. I was 52 years old, definitely old enough to be Black Barbee's father. Prison had warped my sense of reality where every day I woke up thinking that I'm still in my early 30s, or late 20s some days. I needed to get back to reality and break that thought process. I was going to end up just being friends with Black Barbee, and if she considered me a friend, then so be it. I had no problem with that.

When I got into the gift shop, I saw that they had a Chik-Fil-A connected to it. I bought two cobb salads and two lemonades, and as I paid for it, I couldn't help but wonder if the lady behind the register was flirting with me. She was smiling at me, but then again, maybe she was just smiling.

"Good day ma'am." I said as I nodded my head.

"Good day yourself handsome."

I was too old to be blushing, but her infectious charm brought it right out of me. "Thank you." I said. "You're beautiful yourself." I was trying to be nice, but it was true— she was beautiful, but she looked just as young as Black Barbee. If Black Barbee was out of the question, then I knew she would be as well.

"That's you ain't it Terrance?" She said with a huge smile on her face, and moisture in her eyes.

"Huh? You know me?" I was astonished at first, then I realized that a lot of people knew me from the affiliations with my son's record label. I was getting to become like Drake's dad these days.

"You know I know you Terrance. You and me fooled around years back. You don't remember me?"

With that info, I looked at her again, my mind racing and toggling through events; narrowing down on moments.

"Vanessa Croplin?"

"Yes! I'm glad you remember me! I'm standing here feeling the fool for a moment! Come give me a hug!" When she walked around the counter and wrapped her arms around me, it was one of the most refreshing and sensual encounters I'd had since coming home from prison. Granted I'd had my share of thots and groupies, but it never had any emotion other than lust present in the dealings. The embrace I was sharing with Vanessa had the aroma of old friendship, the presence of peace and real affection.

"I could never forget you Vanessa. Wow... You look so good. You've been keeping yourself up really well."

"You look great as well old man." She smiled. "I guess I've been living stress-free, giving all my problems to God."

"God sure took them then because you're more fine today than you was back in the day– and you was sho' nuff fine back then." I wasn't trying to spit game; I was letting her know the absolute truth.

"Thank you so much! I appreciate that! Wow... It's been so long Terrance. When did you get out?"

"It's been a few months now, going on a year."

"That's amazing! God is good!"

"True. God really is wonderful."

"Yes! Yes! You should take my number Terrance. Call me sometimes, I want you to come join my church."

I sighed internally. I didn't remember that part of her. I remember her telling me to call her after school back in the day so I could take her down through there. I reluctantly pulled my phone out and clicked add contact so I could store her information. As she called out her number, I heard a difference in the tone of her voice compared to when she first gave me her phone number back in the day. I glanced at her hand to see if she was married, and noticed it was bare.

"What's your number as well Terrance? I'd love for you to join our church. Are you saved Terrance?"

"Huh?"

"Are you saved?"

I didn't even know what that meant. I stared at her without speaking for a second, then I swallowed. Being behind bars for so long, I found myself constantly learning new slang, new ways to break the law, new mistakes that criminals are making, and new ways to beat the system. I wasn't well versed with church terminology... Not that I didn't believe in God, because I did, but because for the hopeless– the unspoken thought of all of us is that we didn't matter to God. We were the misfits that He didn't acknowledge much or care about. We were the ones he was most disappointed in, so He allowed for us to be separated from the world that He loved. He was going to punish us again once we died. I didn't know how to answer her simple question, or what it even meant.

She grabbed my palm with both of her hands and smiled at me. "Please give me a call Terrance. At your earliest convenience."

She had a calm and nurturing tone in her voice– one that made me want to call her for real, but as soon as I walked out of the gift shop, my mind shifted back to Black Barbee and her fine ass. She was just as flawless as any woman I'd ever laid my eyes on. Body, face, voice, style...

I took the elevator back to the floor where her room was, and when I got there, there was another guy at the counter with flowers in his hand. He had roses, a bear, and what looked like some fruit edibles as well as a brown paper bag. He left the counter and walked into the same room I was headed to. He was in there at least 10 seconds before me, and by the time I got in the room, Black Barbee was awake and smiling at the man.

I stood in the doorway, frozen in my tracks. The man had the initial appearance of old junky with his unkempt hair, but he was definitely young. He had on skinny jeans, some designer shoes, a gold chain, and tats all over his body. When he turned to face me, I realized that I was no match for this young man. Even though his hair was a mess, and his hygiene didn't seem as perfect as it could have been, he looked like one of those underwear models that women swoon after.

"What's up Pops?" He said to me. "Is this your daddy Barbee?"

Black Barbee seemed to focus on me for a second, and then it all came back to her. She looked back up at the man who was questioning her. "Wait... Get the fuck out of my room nigga. Don't you ever contact me again what the fuck!?"

"Bitch you're bi-polar! You was just hugging me and telling me you miss me!"

"Nigga I just remembered what the fuck you did. Get the fuck out of here."

"Huh? I didn't do anything. You had a bad dream Barbee. I've been here right by your side the whole time."

Barbee seemed to be trying to recall something. She furrowed her forehead as squinted her eyes up as she stared at him. "I don't know... Just leave me for now. I'll call you."

"Baby I don't wanna leave your side." He said.

I stepped in, both out of protection of her as a potential friend, and protection of an asset to our record label. "She said leave youngin."

"Who the *fuck* you think you talking to old fool?" He turned to face me, his model looks replaced by the look of the devil.

I placed the bags on the nearby table and was about to go beat his ass like I'd do any of them young niggaz who talked to me crazy in prison, when a security guard came in with a nurse standing beside him.

"Is there a problem?" The guard asked.

"He was just leaving!" Barbee said as she pointed to the young guy.

He looked at her and grinned. Then he looked at me and the security guard and frowned. "Yea... I was just leaving so I wouldn't have to beat two old niggaz up in the hospital."

He walked out as if he owned the world, making sure to stare at me as if his eyes were beaming fear into my soul. It was actually beaming humor, because I knew I could kill that nigga with my bare hand. The other hand I would be recording it on a cell phone the way these other dumb ass niggaz be doing when they post every damn thing on social media.

"I'm sorry OG." Barbee said as she shifted in the hospital bed.

"No it's ok. It's fine."

"That's my ex-nigga. He... Yea... Anyways... What brings you to the hospital? Hell what brings me to the hospital?"

I was about to just tell her she OD'd, but the nurse stopped me. "Leave us alone for a second please. You can sit in the visiting area, and I'll let you know when it's ok for her to have a visitor again. Thank you for understanding."

I took a deep breath and looked at the security guard, who was standing there waiting on me to get the hell out. I looked at Black Barbee, who managed a brief and weak smile, and turned to leave.

"OG." Barbee said as I was halfway out the door. I turned and looked at her, admiring her beauty every chance I got.

"Yes?"

"Thank you." She said before the guard turned to leave out, which was his way of telling me to give them their privacy. He shut the door as he walked out and stood beside the door with his foot on the wall and his hands crossed.

I walked to the visiting area and sat down, mentally replaying the events that had taken place with me and Black Barbee's ex boyfriend. I wondered how our exchange of words made me look to her, and if she saw me as weak— I also wondered what was up with her ex-boyfriend for talking to me like he was fuckin' crazy. I made a mental note to follow up with that situation later. I sat in the corner of the room so I could see each and every person who walked into the area in case anything jumped off. I was on high alert like I was in prison... some things just never changed.

◈

I'd messed around and fallen asleep when I was supposed to be on high alert. I'd been awake for so long that I probably would have still been sleeping if Devin hadn't have called my phone.
"Dad."
"Yes Devin? I'm at the hospital." I said looking around, regaining my bearings. "I'm in the waiting room, waiting on the nurse to let me back to see Black Barbee."
"Hey that's cool Pops, yea I do want you to handle that, but I got something else I want you to handle too."
"Aight. What's up?"
"Have you been paying attention to social media today?"
"I checked it out earlier, but they were talking about the Me Too movement. I think they said something about Russell Simmons—"
"Fuck Russell Simmons. I'm talking about that bitch ass nigga Drum Killer dropping a diss song about me and talking crazy about my family."
Anger immediately flushed through me when I heard the stress in my son's voice. I know he was just like me... He didn't play that shit with nobody, no nigga, nowhere, no type of way. I know he'd been trying to change, but we didn't do diss songs. We didn't do battle raps and hip hop feuds on this side.
"Say no more. I'm leaving the hospital right now!"
"Wait Pops. Finish handling your business with Black Barbee first. Put let's figure out the solution to this shit in the next 24 hours."
"Say no more."
I hung the phone up and stood up to leave. I know he said handle the situation with Black Barbee first, but that wasn't my

style. Beef came before anything, and it would always be that way for me until I'd withdrawn my last breath from this earth. I started walking towards the elevator and was about to press the button to go down when the door opened.

"Barbee... I thought... They let you go already?" I was so confused.

"They didn't have a fuckin' choice. I'm not about to sit in no hospital for that. Shit I've OD'd alone before and woke up fine." Her voice was ragged and low, as if she'd just gotten through arguing with one of the nurses.

I didn't even know how to reply to that. I had a million different emotions circulating all at the same time. "Well... Uhm... For starters... I wanna' say that Q Mack is offering you a $250,000 signing bonus, and 40% of your royalties for 3 years. For the signing bonus, we would need your signature and your bank account and routing number. It shouldn't take long for the money to—"

"Fine. Where do I sign?"

"Wait. The other thing is... You can't be doing the drugs you're using... You gotta pick a different way to ease your mind. A different drug, a different vice."

Black Barbee shifted the weight from one foot to the other. "A different vice like what? My life is so fucking boring, that this is the only thing I can do to decorate it."

"I mean... do you drink? Smoke weed? Have you ever tried a pill? Anything but crack."

Barbee shook her head as if my suggestions were weak and pitiful. "I tried weed, but it's boring too... And if weed is boring and it's illegal in a lot of places, then I know alcohol is going to be boring because it's legal."

I laughed at her logic. "Alright... Look... My son wants me to stick to you like glue. He wants me to make sure you have everything you need, and he wants to make sure I have you in the studio getting this new music recorded. So in a sense, I'll be like your manager, your adviser, your bodyguard- your partner-in-crime if you will. So any moment where you feel so bored that you feel the need to hit a crack rock, just let me fix the moment the best way you can. We can't afford you dying on us with this kind of money on the line."

Barbee had a perplexed look on her face. "You mean... you'll be like a probation officer?"

My facial expression went from nice to ruthless. "I ain't no muthafuckin probation officer. I ain't-"

"I'm just joking. Sheesh." Barbee had a genuine smile on her face, and seeing her smile calmed me down. "So if you're going to be my partner-in-crime... That means if it's something I wanna do or try, you gotta do or try it too right?"

I swallowed. My mind raced briefly, but at the end of the day; I didn't see what the worst was that could happen. I knew I wasn't going to try no crack cocaine, so she could flush that idea. That was out of the question, nor was I going to let her have access to that shit. I couldn't allow my son's investment to go down the drain with her foolishness, and I definitely wasn't going to allow that ex-boyfriend of hers to come through and try to finesse a muthafuckin thing on this side.

"Shit... Yea I'll try some stuff, but I can't try everything."

It didn't seem possible, but Barbee's smile grew even larger. She was grinning ear to ear, lost in the conversation until the elevator buzzed from us holding the door open for so long.

"Aight cool. Where do I sign, and what do we do next?"

It was my turn to smile. I knew I was going to make my son proud the same way he'd made me proud. He'd done so much for me and my life, that I couldn't wait to return the favor however I could. It was because of him that I even had a life, so since he was the reason why, he would also be the reason that I would lay my life down if I had to.

I pulled my phone out to call my son and was startled when Barbee wrapped her arms around me. Her fragrance and the softness of her perfect body caused a flow of blood to swell in my manhood. Out of respect I tried to push her away.

"I'm sorry... I gotta make this phone call real quick."

"So what? You don't wanna hug me?" Barbee's smile hadn't faded. Her teeth were perfect and her lips were flawless.

"I– I– I do... I just..."

"Well put that phone in your pocket... Put your arms around me and hug me tight..."

Her voice was so sensual, the moment was so powerful... I bent over to tie my shoes to hide my growing erection. While I was tying my shoes, she walked up and pressed against me until her thigh was touching my head. I looked up at her startled.

"I saw it in your eyes when you first looked at me... It's ok..." Barbee said gently.

My heart pounded with the passion of a mad lion. I stood up and stared at her. She was a walking, breathing, living replica of a doll. Nobody could tell she was on any type of drug unless the media reported it, but I knew we could fix her image by having a publicist report that those were alternative facts and that she wasn't on any drugs. It was easy to repair a public image and I would see that it be done.

"You're so beautiful..." I said as I shook my head.

"And the way you look at me... I've never had a man look at me that way before. It turns me on so much... I definitely won't mind you being my partner in crime."

"But... What about our ages? I'm–"

She nodded her head and twisted her lips before interrupting me. "I understand if I'm too young for you... but I really have an old soul, and I'm willing to learn whatever you feel I need to be taught. I don't wanna seem like a burden or come off as dead weight... I just genuinely like you."

Her reply shocked me. That just goes to show that insecurity came in all forms and in all people. Nobody on earth was perfect with their thoughts or ways, and there were always mental obstacles present for every level that we were trying to climb to. For her, it seemed as if she'd dated worthless men for so long, that she found herself trying to explain her value to a man who already knew her worth. She didn't have to explain anything to me, nor could anybody ever explain the valuation of something another person saw as priceless.

"I genuinely like you too."

OG

※

After taking Barbee to the lawyer's office to get the business handled, we went and got some food and ate it at my downtown penthouse. I didn't have to tell her to make herself at home because as soon as she got in the door she started picking up clothes I had laying around. We talked a little bit about life, and I asked her if she wanted to stay or if she felt more comfortable being in a hotel room by herself. She didn't reply, instead she went into my bedroom and started cleaning up more– which I finally put two and two together and realized that she had no intentions on leaving.

I had some intentions on leaving though because I had work to do in the streets. I'd since heard the song that Drum Killer had done dissing my son, and I couldn't stand for that. My throat had been tight all day while plotting on getting revenge on that fuck nigga.

"Barbee. I have to go handle some things, but I'll be back soon ok?"

"Ahhh ok... You're leaving me already? I thought we were going to have some fun? I thought you were going to get drunk with me since it'll be my first time?"

It sounded so tempting, but not as tempting as busting that nigga's head. "I tell you what... Let's skip the alcohol tonight, and how about tomorrow we take a vacation to Las Vegas? Maybe I can see if Q Mack doesn't have plans and wants to go with us. That'll be a great escape for all of us, and it'll also give you a chance to meet your boss. What do you think?"

"I'd love to go to Las Vegas! I've never been anywhere. Ever."

"Well with me you're going to see the world. I got you."

"Okay!" Her smile was infectious. "Now hurry back Zaddy."

Something about her words put a spark under me. Something about her wanting to stay at my penthouse did something to me emotionally. Something about having someone who liked me arose feelings that I never knew I had. It felt like my soul was resurrecting— like I was alive again, like I was finally getting a chance to live after being dead to the world for so many years.

I never once thought that I would be out of prison with full access to not only my dream life but to the woman of my dreams as well. I never knew I could be able to live life without worrying about money or finances, that I would be able to have the type of platform and opportunities handed to me the way my son had done for me. I was truly blessed and thankful, but at the same time I knew there was a part of me that would never change. That nigga was going to die for disrespecting my son and my family. We didn't play that shit and we never would. There were people who would happily play those types of games, but that's where we differed from other men. We would die for what we believed in.

※

There was a part of me that was down-right rotten and demented. A part of me that nobody knew the depths of except for the best of my friends, and my son. He'd watched my demeanor enough in the past year or so to know that I was just like him. It was a part of me that was all-white-sheet dreams, all ambitions of seeing my enemy resting peacefully in a casket– a part of me that wanted to volunteer as a grave digger and pallbearer free of charge to make sure that that body was lowered into the ground at the correct depth.

It was a part of me that was lifeless. A deep, dark part of me that was death walking and breathing, a section of my soul that had no evidence that God had created it. A living devil when provoked– an angel whenever love was present, and the angel of hell whenever hatred was in the building. I didn't go looking for enemies, nor did I create tension with or randomly attack strangers. My only obligation was to see my family members happy and breathing, and it meant that I would enact whatever level of penalty on whoever decided to attempt to take the happiness away from the ones that I loved.

I had a pistol in my possession, but I didn't plan on firing it. Many rookie criminals didn't understand that the reason they got caught up on so many murder charges was because of the mess that a pistol made whenever it was fired. Shell case matches, fingerprints, blood splatter remnants that was only visible under certain lights that the police owned, gun powder remnants– any criminal firing a gun was one who was ready to go to prison.

I had a large pistol, but it was only for paralysis. A typical person stopped in his tracks when they saw a barrel pointed at them. A paralyzed person was helpless already, so what was the point of firing a gun? I'm too old school, too smart for that; that's something I would have to leave for the young dummies of the world.

It didn't take me long to find the whereabouts of Drum Killer that night. These young niggaz be on Instagram acting like they have beef, yet they be posting their whereabouts all night because they're not used to having real consequences for their actions. These men grew up with no fathers, and when they reached a certain age, their mothers weren't able to penalize them correctly—therefore they felt like consequences didn't apply to them.

I was waiting outside of the studio that Drum Killer was recording at that night. He'd made a post of him doing a collab with a new female artist, so I knew based on their body language in the Instagram video post that he was going to try to fuck her once he left the studio. And since I knew this, I also knew that he wasn't going to have any bodyguards or niggaz around him. Niggaz like that wanted to try to act like they were the man whenever a woman was present. There was no way to come off as an alpha male if you had niggaz watching your back like a got damn supervisor. This nigga had a bright yellow Ferrari parked in the parking lot, so I knew I could park a half mile away and not lose this hot ass nigga. Shit was a joke really.

I waited until I saw them walk outside. They'd been holding hands until they stepped out of the building, then they tried to act cordial in case paparazzi were out snapping pictures. I sat in the car and watched them for a while, and after long Drum Killer pulled off in his Ferrari. I let him pull off, and instead I followed the chick. She would be unsuspecting and less paranoid because she hadn't done shit and didn't have beef with anybody. She was just looking for a come up, so she wouldn't even be looking in her rear view while thinking only about the future. She just didn't know that her future was right behind her with a sinister grin on his face.

I followed her all the way up into Cobb county, but I was several car lengths behind her just in case she did feel like someone was following her. She turned into a place called Garden Lakes, which was a residential sub-division. I didn't even follow her. It was pointless. I was going to wait until she left and pull up into the sub-division until I spotted his loud ass Ferrari. He was trying to stunt for that bitch, so I knew he wasn't going to have the Ferrari in the garage. He was probably going to have half of his fleet parked in the driveway. Niggaz like him wasn't going to make it on my watch.

I drove down the street and parked inside of a self-service car wash station. I opened the door by the vacuum, but I wasn't trying to clean my car out, I was only trying to get my dirt together. I had the pistol on deck, the brass knuckles on deck, and the Freddy Kreuger retractable-blade-glove. I had on an all white sauna sweat suit from Gold's Gym, and for good reason.

That nigga must have either bust a quick nut, she had an emergency, or he said something stupid to her because she was out of there not even 20 minutes after she'd arrived. That was my cue. I drove into the sub-division just as soon as she drove out, and just as I thought, that nigga's spot wasn't hard to find at all. He had a convertible Bentley in the drive-way, but little did he know, I was going to show him how to drop a top.

I parked up the street behind a white truck that was parked on the street beside someone's house. The only reason I parked there was because their lawn hadn't been done in a while, so either they didn't give a fuck about shit, or they were in another city on vacation somewhere for the summer. I got out and walked down the street until I got to Drum Killer's steps. I had gloves on, and a ski-mask in my pocket that I wasn't going to use until it was time for me to walk back to my car.

I rang his doorbell and waited patiently. I rang it again, and finally I heard the door locks unlatch. As he was unlocking the other lock, he took the time to engage in conversation from behind the door.

"I figured you were going to come back and gimme that pussy. You had to think about it huh? Shit I'm a rich nigga, what other option you got unless you like fuckin' all those lames you been out here—"

When he opened the door I had a barrel in his face. His mouth dropped open and his eyes opened wide. I could smell the bitch fragrance coming off of his skin. Bitch fragrance was heat activated, and there was nothing hotter in life than the barrel of a large pistol. He may have called himself drum killer, but he'd never killed a got damn thing in his entire life. He knew who I was, it was evident on his face, and since he knew who I was, then he also had to know what I was there for.

"I'm so– I'm– I'm sorry I–"

I walked in and jammed the barrel in his mouth. His eyes opened wide and stared straight up in the sky as if a dentist was pulling a tooth. "Who's here with you nigga?" I asked. I didn't have time to play and no room for mistakes. "If you lie to me, nigga you're dead in the fuckin water. So don't lie."

He shook his head but didn't move the direction of his eyes. I pulled the barrel out of his mouth and pressed it against his chest. "I said who's fucking here with you king!"

"No- Nobo- Nobody's here! Pl- please don't kill me! Pl- Please I- I won't-"

I slid my right hand in my pocket and enclosed them into the slots of the brass knuckles. I pulled my hand out of my pocket and he didn't even see it coming.

Wham! The impact of the brass knuckles laid him on the floor with one punch. He crawled backwards in a bloody daze and fell, but he didn't get far crawling. The next blow was hard enough to give him brain damage, as I struck him with the impact of a truck going 100 miles an hour in a head-on collision. I swung with the power of a home-run hitter, and hit him two more times for good measure.

The power I'd hit him with using the brass knuckle was enough to kill an elephant, but I wasn't done. I wasn't about to explain to him what he'd done wrong or play all those games them niggaz be playing in the movies and on television. On TV, niggaz get in the house and have all that talking going on. Niggaz don't be killers for real, they be counselors. Shit I wasn't no fuckin counselor. If I didn't wanna talk to you when you was living, why talk when I'm about to take your life. Fuck you nigga.

For good measure, I pulled out the retractable Freddy Kreuger glove, pressed one button and four extra sharp blades erected themselves out like deadly fingernails. It took one swipe for me to turn his throat into the top of a salt shaker. The splatter from the impact splashed on my white sauna suit. I was going to set it on fire before I left his place. It was thin so it was going to melt with no effort. Under the sauna suit I had on a white jogging suit that I wasn't going to melt or burn. It was going to be the suit I walked back and got into my car with. It was going to be the flawless suit that I would allow the forensic team to seize from me if it ever came down to it, but I doubt it would ever come to that.

I finished up my job in less than 20 minutes, and I was back in my car about to finish up my night before I headed back to my Buckhead penthouse. I'd made sure not to make any mistakes with the murder, and the only thing I had to do at that point was get rid of the brass knuckles in one place and dump the Freddy Kreuger knife somewhere else. I had a beautiful woman at my spot that I couldn't wait to be in the presence of. I drove about 10 miles until I found a landfill, but it had a razor gate around it almost like a prison housing complex.

I knew I wasn't about to break in there just to hide a weapon, so I kept driving until I got to Piedmont Road. There was a large dumpster sitting at an angle across from the Smashburger, and after I wrapped the brass knuckles in newspaper and placed them inside of a plastic bag, I tossed it and went on about my business. I was going to figure out what to do with the glove at a later time. My current task was to find out what I was gon do with Black Barbee's fine ass.

I made it back to my Penthouse and parked. I felt amazing, truly wonderful about life and all of the opportunities I had. I walked down the hallway en route to the elevator and stopped in front of a full body mirror. I frowned when I saw my face. The self esteem crept out of my body when the mirror read me my truths. The truth was that I was just an old man who gave away his best years in prison. The truth was that I wasn't desirable, I had greys— I was in position to get a bottle of liquor with no ID for the rest of my life.

In prison, they removed the mirrors for a few reasons. For one, they didn't want us to use them as weapons, and for two, they didn't want us to see how many years the system was stealing from us. Now that I was free, the image of being a victim of oppression was razor sharp. There was no reason for me to believe that I could keep Black Barbee's attention as her success sky-rocketed, but I was definitely down to try. The only thing that mattered right now was that I knew she liked me, and I definitely liked her too. I made a promise to myself to continue living by the rules I lived by in prison— stop worrying about the things I was unable to control, and go all out for the things I could.

ASHLON

I loved my husband dearly. I loved him deeper than anything I'd ever loved in this lifetime. The way he kissed me, the way he protected me and the kids, the gentleman he was to us, the way he made loved to me, and even the way he opened my straw for me when we ordered fast food. It was incredible how positive of a change I'd witnessed him exhibit for the sake of our family. He was the perfect man for me... but some times I prayed extra hard because some days... I didn't feel I was the perfect woman for him.

   I often prayed and asked God if I deserved to have a husband so good, and if I did indeed deserve to have one so amazing, to please send me the signs necessary so that I could stop worrying about it being snatched away from me at any given moment. Even though I was on the Forbes list and had such an extremely successful company, underneath it all was a woman who had to crouch over her daughter in the freezing rain to prevent her from being sick.

   Under it all was a woman who was homeless and had no support from family and no support from her daughter's father. So imagine my surprise when he called me that morning...

"Hello?"

"Junior?" I really was at a loss for words. This nigga had made absolutely no effort to be in his daughter's life, and here he was calling me for a change.

"How's Ayeeka?"

How's Ayeeka? Nigga what? This is the first time you've ever asked about Ayeeka you bastard. I had a million thoughts going through my mind and all of them were negative except for my response.

"Ayeeka's fine... What's up?"

"That's good... I'm glad she's doing well... I wanna spend time with her if that's possible. Soon..."

I frowned. Exploded inside. Stabbed him mentally. Shot him in my imagination and regurgitated on his body. Hated him forever in my head, killed him in a thousand dreams and volunteered to dig his grave in many of my daydreams... Then I replied...

"Alright... She'll be happy to spend time with you." I don't know why I spoke for her. The truth was I wasn't sure how she would feel, but I didn't want to build a child up learning how to hate when all she understood was love.

"Good. I can't wait."

I didn't know why Junior was calling me out of the blue, and suddenly wanting to be in his child's life, but it really didn't matter to me what his reason was. What mattered to me was the fact that a part of me felt validated, valued, and important. The hungry part of me that always wondered why he never gave a fuck about his child was suddenly faced with the opportunity for a plate.

A part of me wanted to flaunt my wins in front of him so I could show him what he'd lost. I couldn't wait to take his daughter to see him, so I could see the regret in his face when he stared at me. My glow up was for moments like this, because I always knew that my time was coming. He was going to be super disappointed when he realized he couldn't get to me mentally. I was a married woman and he'd had countless opportunities to secure me back in the day, but he didn't want me. I was going to make sure that he understood my damn glow.

"Well... Junior, when do you wanna see her?"

"Are you in Atlanta?"
"Yea."
"Well, what about now?"
"What? Now?" It was 7:30 AM and my husband was still sleeping. I was in the kitchen finishing up breakfast and there was no way I would do such a thing. It just didn't make sense to me. Then a voice inside me kept pushing me to capture my validation... I hated that I felt like that. I'd been wronged by this man continuously so his opinions shouldn't have mattered to me in any form or fashion, but I couldn't help it... It was my human nature to wanna prove that I never needed him and that he was in the wrong. *Shit...*
"Hello?" Junior asked, after the brief silence.
"Oh I'm here. Uhm... Yea I can't leave right now. I'll have to wait until my husband wakes up." Inside a part of me was clapping and cheering my reply. *You go bitch!* I smiled while waiting his response.
"Oh. Alright. I guess I understand then."
"Yea."
"Well... after he gets up, just let me know. I'll be around and available for whenever."
I snapped out of my daze of seeking validation just that quick. It was way too early in the morning for the devil to be trying me, and I was going to show his ass that I was a stronger woman than I was yesterday. It only takes one bad error or lapse in judgment to ruin even the strongest of relationships, just like it only takes one hole in a boat to sink it, and just like even the slightest of error on the expressway could lead to an accident. In a world of numbers, people often underestimated the power of one.
"Yea, well; whenever my husband can get free to bring us to meet you is when I'll be available. Ok?"
He snickered.
"What's funny?"
"What's not?"
"Man you called me, I didn't call you. I don't have time for games, I have breakfast to cook for my family. Is there anything—"

"Chill, chill. I didn't mean anything by it. I admire your growth. You're doing good. Just hit me if you ever need me."

He hung up just as randomly as he'd called me. I dropped to my knees in the kitchen and prayed. I had things I needed resolve from, and it couldn't wait another moment.

"Dear Father Jesus... First I would like to ask for forgiveness for all sins that I've done or contributed in, both knowingly and unknowingly. I would like to ask for protection against all desires of my flesh, all desires of my spirit that don't belong in your realm of standards. I don't want to seek revenge God, I only wanna seek you. I don't wanna find retaliation in my heart, I only wanna find you in my heart. I pray to you God..."

The tears fell when I felt the tension being pulled out of me. God was a great God. He was so amazing and perfect, so mighty and He was always there for me. I was so thankful that I was able to pass the test of the devil, but I was sure to be tested again; and I prayed that whenever it came I aced it with the blessings of my teacher, the Almighty.

"Baby you ok?"

The sound of my husband's voice made my tears flow harder. He was in the kitchen in his boxers and t-shirt, and he never came out of the room like that when the girls were in the house so I know that the spirit made him get up to comfort me. It was no other way. I tried to get up off of the knees to hug him, but he pressed my right shoulder, signaling for me to go back down. He joined me and got on his knees beside me. In life, I've learned that some things can't be stopped— death, taxes, bills, and my tears...

"Father God."

My husband's voice sounded like an explosion into the depths of my soul. Some people loved the sound of jazz music and some people enjoyed the sound of the ocean. To me, even though my husband made great music and had a tremendously wonderful talent, nothing on this planet sounded greater than my husband in prayer.

"We come to you on this morning humbly and respectfully. We come as we are, flawed and of your creation, and we ask for help to be better of your

grace. We hurt and we cry, we make mistakes but we still try... I ask that you bless our family, allow us the strength to forever love each other in your grace. Allow me the chance to grow to be a better man for my wife, a better father to my kids, a better son for you my Father. I've made mistakes God... I let my feelings get the best of me so many times... I try to fight the urge and I try to be better... I pray to you for forgiveness and I ask that you handle my enemies so that they no longer get to me. I thank you for my wife, for my praying woman— What else could I possibly ask from you, knowing you've given me the absolute best cards in the deck? Bless her further God. Bless her business and her spirit, and cover her in the sprinkles of your glow. God I thank you for everything. In Jesus Christ's name I pray. Amen."

I put my arms around my husband and kissed him passionately.
"I love you Devin."
"I love you too Ashlon."

It was these words that we never failed to give to each other. There was never a day when we didn't speak it. Sometimes I would say those words and know that they weren't strong enough to really explain how I felt.

My husband stood up and pulled me up. He kissed me on the forehead and smiled, then walked back to the room and went back to sleep. I had been in the process of making dough to make biscuits before the phone call, and I made a point to get back to it after washing my hands. I turned the radio on using the app on my phone and started listening to the A Town Morning Show.

I started nodding my head as I listened to a love song by a singer that featured my husband. It was a new song that I'd never heard before, and even though I was only able to catch the end of it I knew it was going to be a hit. The music faded out and I thought my phone had died for a quick second before hearing the DJ's voice.

"Let's have a moment of silence for the young rapper Drum Killer, who was found slain early this morning. A relative living with him made the call to 911 about his murder, no word yet on if she saw what happened or if there are any suspects. A tragedy for the Hip Hop community. As you know, not even a few days ago

Drum Killer shocked us all with the diss song about legendary rapper Q Mack Money— which probably has nothing to do with this situation, but as you all know about Q Mack's past with his old murder for hire charges and—"

"You're reaching." Her co-host told her.

"You're right, you're right. Well I definitely just would like to send my condolences to the family of Drum Killer, and we would like to ask the public for a moment of silence for this sad tragedy."

I turned my phone off and my hands started shaking as the anger gripped my body like a glove. I was angry that they wouldn't let my husband's past stay in the past. Every time something happened, they threw it up as if they were without sin and had no skeletons in their own Fashion Nova filled closets. We were constantly being attacked by the media, and although it wasn't fair to us, we were going to make it no matter what.

I struggled to make the dough that morning. Normally the biscuits would be perfectly round, the precise shape of a doughnut; but that morning the biscuits were probably going to come out looking like the shape of a ragged starfish. Cooking usually reflected my energy, and that morning it was right back in tatters after listening to the way the media was going to try to throw my husband's name into the bs. I hated that for him. He fought so hard and so much, and in my opinion I didn't think he deserved the fights that kept coming his way. I took a deep breath and told myself it was going to be ok. *We...* were going to be just fine.

BARBEE

Life was just as incredible and amazing as it was difficult. The last 36 hours had shown me an entire new angle to living. I woke up and checked my Wells Fargo bank account and was floored when the computerized voice read the balance out to me. Over a quarter million dollars just for signing my signature on a contract was something I would have never imagined could have happened for me. All of the days I struggled and begged God to help me, I never thought that it was going to happen in this magnitude.

My heart was full and my soul felt a thousand times lighter than normal. It was as if God had opened the curtains of my dark spirit and allowed his Glory to shine in. OG was laying next to me sleeping. I respected him even more because he didn't try me last night, and I slept stark naked in his bed. He simply came back in, showered and cuddled with me until he fell asleep. He'd already had my respect just for being there for me in my time of misery, but now he had my full attention.

Our conversation was fluent— a conversation with someone who you're not supposed to be with will be like broken English, but in the past I would accept broken English as opposed to getting no communication at all. I guess I needed to know broken

English so I know the difference— and now I could identify fluent perfection whenever it was presented to me. I had music on my heart, and no desire for drugs right then, which was rare. I usually woke up needing to burn that demon and inhale it in smoke format.

"Good morning." Terrance's voice was groggy, and his eyes were still closed.

"Morning baby." I said trying to suppress the happiness in my voice. I didn't wanna seem over-excited, but the facts were... I was more excited than I'd ever been in my life. So many people had let me down, yet here I was... up.

"Let's get dressed so we can go get breakfast." Terrance said as he rolled over to check the time. "Do you have anything to wear?"

"Yes, I have a pair of shorts and tank top in my bag."

He smiled. "Cool, put that on, then let's go to Lenox Mall so I can take you shopping for our Vegas trip."

I'd never had a man take me shopping my entire life. Not my father, not a boyfriend— so I'd never experienced even hearing those words come from a man. I couldn't wait because it was something I dreamed of happening to me. I'd read so many books and seen so many movies where men did it for their women, but I didn't feel it would ever happen to me... until then.

I got up and went to the bathroom. Waking up to go shopping and get breakfast was a big difference between getting up and shopping for something to smoke. I was grateful for the transformation in my life, but the unfortunate fact was that an addiction is no different from hunger. If you haven't eaten anything the whole day, you'll feel an empty feeling and your stomach will begin to hurt. That's how it was with most addictions, and it's why so many people can't go without disappointing the ones that they loved. For the moment however, I was going to try my best to change. I could tell that Terrance really cared for me... but the reality of it was that he didn't really know the real me.

Once he got to learn the real me and my genuine tendencies, would he still adore me the way he did now? Would he still wake me up for breakfast and shopping once he'd gotten what he wanted from me? It all remained to be seen. Many men liked me— I knew I was beautiful despite my addiction, and I knew I was blessed with talent despite my demons. This was a combination to attract men of all types, but for one to overlook my flaws and work with me to try to make me be a better person was the only thing I was interested in.

It was a difference between love and lust, like and love, and hurt and pain. I'd experienced all of them except for love, and I was praying that it was time.

OG TERRANCE

Since we'd decided to go shopping first, we skipped breakfast and went straight to brunch at the Cheese Cake Factory. I enjoyed making Barbee smile, and I could see myself spending the rest of my days with her although I barely knew her. I liked the way she chewed food, the way she took charge when the waitress came over and ordered my food as well, the way she picked the napkin up and wiped my chin and lip for me as I ate. I liked the way she double checked the receipts every time I made a purchase. I liked the way she made me open my burger so she could see if it was cooked properly. The way she cared for me let me know that I could freely do the same for her without worry.

I was staring at her in amazement of her presence. In full appreciation of this fine specimen of a woman. In love with the contours of her face, the shape of her nose, the edge of her hair, the depth of darkness in her eye brows... Fascination by the perfect arrangement of a woman. I couldn't recall a time I'd been in the presence of a woman so beautiful.

My phone rang and I frowned at the interruption. I exhaled and answered.

"Hello?"

"Hey Terrance! How are you? Have you gave it any thought about joining our church? I was telling the Pastor about you this morning, as you've been on my spirit heavy since we ran into each other at the hospital. You should join our church! Do you wanna talk to the Pastor sometime today? After you join our church maybe we can go grab a bite to eat and catch up with old times!"

I felt like hanging up on her but I wouldn't do her like that. Instead I was going to have to save her number as *Do Not Answer* so I could continue to have my peace. She was definitely bothering me at that point by continuously trying to pitch her church off to me.

"Yea lemme call you back."

I hung the phone up and met Barbee's calming smile with my own. Before I could speak the phone rang again. I exhaled harder, but relaxed once I saw it was my son calling.

"Excuse me Barbee... I have to take this call." I said as I placed my credit card on the table and stood up to walk to the front of the restaurant. Our business was ultra private, and I couldn't afford to discuss it in front of anybody.

"Hello?"

"Dad what's up?" Devin said, and I could hear irritation in his voice.

"I'm relaxing. I'm happy. I took Barbee to eat and things can't be better. We're–"

"Uhm yea I know you took Barbee out, and you would know that the whole world knows it too since The Shade Room posted pictures that a fan took of you two eating at The Cheese Cake Factory. I thought I told you to start keeping up with Instagram?"

I hated that I felt like I was letting my son down. "Damn. I'm sorry Devin. You know this is all new to me and I keep forgetting to check it."

"Forgetting is unacceptable Dad. I told you this was important, and at this point I feel like you're ignoring me and you're using this *being new to you* as an excuse."

"That's really the last thing I'm trying to do Devin. I apologize and I promise to do better."

"If you had been checking, then you'd know that they found the rapper dead this morning."

"Yea. And what? I don't care. That's their job, they're supposed to find his ass."

"Yea and if you'd have done your job, you'd have known that somebody was in the house with him!"

Panic stopped me from breathing. How stupid and lazy had I been to not check the house instead of taking his word for it. I was punching myself in the face in my mind for making such a stupid rookie mistake.

"Shit Devin... Man I..."

"I don't wanna hear it. You made the error, so you keep the same energy of that error if you ever have to face it in the future. If you couldn't do it right, then you shouldn't have done it at all. There were plenty of people—"

"I got it son. It's going to be fine. I promise you... Don't worry."

"Aight... well now that that's out of the way... How's Barbee doing? Have y'all made studio arrangements?"

"She's fine Devin. I was wondering... How about we all go on a vacation to Las Vegas? You and your wife haven't really taken a break from work since y'all got married, and I was thinking we could all use this trip to re-invigorate and infuse our motivation. You know when Phil Jackson was coaching the Chicago Bulls back in the day, he would do things to motivate his team outside of just practicing in the basketball gym. It worked out when the Bulls won 72 games and only lost 10 that year."

"Hmm... Aight... And let me guess... You're bringing Black Barbee?" Devin asked with a smile apparent in his voice. It was the first time he'd shown any type of emotion besides anger and concern since we'd been on the phone.

"I'm bringing her so you could meet her... It's just business son. I'm going to make sure to handle business first."

"Yea ok. Well aight... Let me check with the baby-sitter and if she can take care of the girls for a few days. I've been to Las Vegas to do shows and concerts, but I never did anything in the city, and I always told myself that I was going to see what some of these places had to offer besides sold out shows. Aight... We can do that Pops."

I smiled. Despite the error I'd made with not checking the house, I had a great feeling that everything was going to be just fine. I couldn't wait to get to Las Vegas. I'd been reading about that city for years while I was in prison, and it was on my bucket list to go whenever I was financially in position to afford such a trip. There was no better time than the present.

THE WATER BALLOON EFFECT

The balloon of life can be compared to a water balloon. Inside of the fragile material is the contents that makes that balloon important to begin with. If you squeeze the water balloon gently, the water will not leave the balloon, but instead will shift to another part of the balloon. If you squeeze that side, it will shift to a part of the balloon with less pressure. In the balloon of life, if you have a bad habit, that particular bad habit may leave, but the root of the habit will simply go elsewhere.

This is the science of replacement. Some replacements you may be familiar with are:

1. *"Find something else to do with your time."*
2. *"Eat a salad instead of eating unhealthy foods."*
3. *"Drink red wine instead of hard liquor."*
4. *"Try a nicotine patch instead of smoking."*
5. *"Drink water instead of soda."*

The science of replacement knows that there still lies the urge to fill whatever habit

that human behavior has formed over time. The science of replacement says that in order for us to be better people, our goals should be to replace our worst habits and focus our attention in other places. The catch to this is that some people have stronger addictive personalities than others, which makes breaking from forming a habit something that has to be identified in the early stages rather than later.

LAS VEGAS

Las Vegas, Nevada was an exceptionally beautiful city. It was the city of freedom, the United States capital of excitement, a rare melting pot of free spirits– both spiritual and alcoholic. A person could come to Las Vegas with the weight of the world on his shoulder, and find themselves quickly forgetting all problems that existed. It was the desert– blazing hot at 107 degrees, but decorated with so much flesh, shiny lights, money, and drugs that your body quickly forgot that it was way too hot for a human to be walking around with a smile on his or her face.

Vegas was alluring. Many came with the idea that whatever happened there, stayed there, and this was true on some accords but not all. The palm trees on the Las Vegas strip looked like they belonged on the beach, the lights looked like they came out of a light show, and the dazzling displays of multi-million-dollar waterworks were sophisticated enough to capture the attention of even the most stone faced visitor.

The small group of four were all wide-eyed as they absorbed the sights en route to Caesar's Palace. Devin had been to Vegas several times for work, but had never gotten a chance to enjoy anything. He was determined to enjoy his trip since they were scheduled to be there for 3 days. He pulled his wife closer to him as he felt inspired by the incredible energy of the city. He was so glad that he'd chosen to listen to his father, and judging by the look on his father's face, he could tell that this was a much needed trip.

"I can't wait to try the slot machines." Black Barbee said as her bright eyes surveyed the scene and absorbed every detail.

"I wanna try my hand at some blackjack. Maybe I'll win me a million dollars." OG Terrance said with a childish grin on his face.

"Babe I wanna see one of the magic shows." Ashlon was giddy also. Everyone had something pre-planned that they always wanted to explore about Las Vegas except Devin.

"What's the first thing you gon do son?" Terrance asked as the small group smiled at him.

"Uhm... I'm not sure honestly... I'm just going to take it as it comes."

"Ain't nothing wrong with that!" Terrance said as he glanced down and sent his phone to voicemail.

"Who was that calling you babe?" Barbee looked at him with a serious face.

"Some lady trying to get me to join a church. That's all. It's time to have fun!" He put the phone in his pocket as the limo pulled up to the front entrance of Caesar's Palace.

The driver hopped out and opened the rear and helped the party of four get out of the limo. He popped the trunk to retrieve their bags, and Devin smiled at the man's great customer service. He reached in his pocket, pulled out a wad of 100s, and peeled a crisp blue note off and handed it to him.

"Thank you sir! Wow. I really appreciate that." The driver said, suddenly feeling like he hadn't done enough to deserve his generousness.

"What's your name?"

"Devin."

"Devin, I'm Todd. Here's my card." He reached in his pocket and pulled his wallet out. He only had one card in his wallet and it was beaten to tatters. It was obvious he didn't use business cards often.

"That's my cell phone number right there on the bottom. I've been living in Las Vegas for 35 years so if it's any questions you have about anything, call me anytime, day or night."

"I appreciate that. I surely will." Devin shook his hand and took 3 steps before the bellman stopped them and took their bags from them.

"After you check in, just bring the ticket to the bell desk and we'll deliver your bags to your rooms."

"Thanks! We bouta go win us some money. Y'all coming?" Terrance said as he pivoted from one foot to the other as if he had to use the bathroom. Barbee had a big grin on her face, it was obvious that she was as excited as she'd ever been, and Devin didn't wanna ruin the vacation by laying down rules.

"Y'all have fun. We'll catch up with y'all later. Me and my wife are about to find something to eat."

"Say no more." OG Terrance said as he made a bee-line towards the casino. He had Barbee's hand in his hand, and Devin smirked while watching the couple.

"Don't you say it." Ashlon said with a smile on her face.

"Ash... I mean... This man old enough to be–"

"Let them be happy Devin. Don't be like that."

"Alright. Alright. You're right. I'm just going to enjoy this trip. I'm sure we'll spend time with them, but the most important thing to me right now is just the two of us." Devin said as he pulled his wife up close to him.

"Just the three of us. But we'll talk about that when we get back home." Ashlon said as she burst out laughing.

"Wait what? Huh?"

"We'll discuss it. Not today. Let's just enjoy."

"Wowww... You're doing that?" Devin started laughing. "I deserve it though. You got it." Even though his heart was beating a thousand times a minute at the possibility of it being *the three* of them, he would respect her wishes and talk about it when they got back home. He couldn't prevent his mind from racing however as he thought about if the new addition was going to be a boy or girl. Either way he was going to be grateful.

"Devin. You ok?"

He had been in a trance just standing outside the casino hotel and didn't even realize it.

"Oh yea baby. I'm great. Let's go check into our rooms so we can grab something to eat."

ASHLON

I really didn't intend on telling Devin about the pregnancy while in Las Vegas, but it just slipped out from trying to hold all of my excitement in. I'd taken a dollar store pregnancy test before we left Atlanta and it showed up positive. I was meaning to get it confirmed with a blood test first, but since the cat was out of the bag, I guess it wasn't so bad.

Our hotel room was something straight out of a dream. My husband told me he booked us a suite, but by the time I walked through the first part of the room, I was convinced that we were in an actual home. It was amazing! Floor to ceiling windows from wall to wall, two bedrooms, 2 bathrooms, a dining room, a living room, play area, study room– by the time I laid on the bed I pretty much knew I was going to be there for a while. It was so soft it felt as if I was laying on air. I'd come a long way from having nowhere to sleep and nobody to run to. The moment I ran to Devin's arms was the moment my whole life changed.

"Baby you ready to get something to eat?" Devin asked when he came out of the bathroom.

I smiled at him. "I think I'll just get room service baby. I'm kinda exhausted from that flight we took."

"Really? You can't fly all the way to Las Vegas and go to sleep. Vegas is the city that never sleeps. We gotta go hard."

"I know baby... Just give me an hour and I'll be ready for all that."

Devin came over to me and sat on the bed beside me.

"You're sleepy too Devin?"

"I'm not, but I'm going to be here for you while you sleep. You know I'm not leaving you."

"Devin. No. Go enjoy yourself. Go get a head start so you can know where to take me. I'll be fine."

"Uhm... I can wait and we can explore it together."

"No Devin, we both can't be party poopers. Remember we have people with us. Make sure they're good. I'll be fine." I could see the reluctance on his face. I knew if I allowed him to, he would lay there with me the whole weekend, and I knew he needed this break more than anybody.

"Alright then." Devin kissed me on the forehead, neck and then crouched down and kissed me on the stomach. I loved that man, and I planned on loving him forever until the end of time. He was patient and perfect, and the way he cared for me was second to none. I'd never been cared for like that in my entire life, and God knew I appreciated his blessings because I told him every day.

I turned my phone back on once Devin left out of the room, in case he or the baby sitter needed to contact me for any reason. I'd forgot to turn it back on from powering it down at the beginning of the 4-hour flight. Once my phone was back on, a continuous stream of text messages flooded through. I glanced at the texts and had to wipe my eyes to double check to make sure I was seeing what I was seeing.

Hey... This is Junior. I know our last conversation didn't go that good, but I still enjoy talking to you. Your voice is still as mesmerizing now as it was when I first met you. I would love to be a part of my daughter's life, and possibly be in your life as well... just as a friend because I respect your marriage.

I gritted my teeth because with the flood of emotions during and after our prayer, the excitement of the pregnancy test and being so happy to pack our bags to leave, I totally forgot to tell Devin about Ayeeka's father contacting me. I was going to tell him, but I didn't want him to make a big deal out of it because I knew it was something I could actually handle on my own. Hell I thought I was doing just fine.

Just let me know when a good time will be for Ayeeka to–

I started typing and stopped. It was pointless for me to keep saying the same thing over and over. I'd told his ass that me and my husband would bring his daughter to see him, but he hadn't said anything concerning when. I sat the phone down and closed my eyes, my mind racing and toggling from thought to thought. I thought about what I would name the baby if it was a girl, or what Devin would want to name the baby if it was a boy. I wondered if he wanted a junior Devin or not. My phone buzzed again, and it was starting to irritate me. I snatched it up about to cuss his ass out.

Ashlon... My mother died last week, and it broke my heart. You don't know the pain I've endured nor the tears I've dropped. It was an eye-opening experience for me, and it made me wake up from all of the tension we've had with each other in the past. I just want to say that I love you and I respect you as a woman. I know I didn't make it easy for you, so I don't expect for you to make it easy for me. Just know that I would like to be your friend in whatever capacity you'll have me. I mean no disrespect to your marriage, but I do know that we're family, and family is all I have left.

The emotional side of me almost let a tear fall out of my eye. Instead I placed the phone face down and got up out of the bed. I'd known his mother and she actually liked me. She was the one trying to talk some sense into her son and telling him that he needed to marry me before he lost me. Old emotions and memories started clouding my conscience, old thoughts from the past seemed to slip its way into the hotel room. Suddenly, as big as the room was; it was starting to seem small to me. I knew life was short, and I knew as a Christian woman that it was my duty to forgive, forget, and move on.

A tear slipped out of my eye even when I didn't want it to happen. That's when I knew that I wasn't about to fake like I didn't care. I did care, not just because he was the father of my child, not just because my child's grandmother passed; but because that was my genetic makeup and my biggest flaw... My heart. I saw a lot of me in Devin and a lot of him in me. I think that's why we connected so strong, and why our love is so deep. As a wife I knew that I shouldn't have forgotten to tell him about Junior contacting me, but as a human being I simply forgot.

I picked the phone up to reply to his text, and thought better against it. As a person in the spotlight, every text I sent out could possibly end up in the public's view, so I decided maybe that wasn't the best thing to do. I'd already replied enough... However, I had to get some things off of my chest so I could properly forgive, and I needed to check to see how he was mentally having had a loss so life-changing. I dialed his number and walked into the bathroom. I stared in the mirror at the old me with intentions to shed the dead skin clouding my newness. A part of me had to let go of the past completely– Letting go of the past meant that at any point if it was ever brought up, I'd be able to handle it appropriately with my actions, emotions, and thoughts. Some people confuse letting go with ignoring, and it's not the same. To let go, it means to drop an entire vehicle in the depths of a hole so big that you could listen all night and never hear a sound.

"Hello."

"Thank you for calling me Ashlon." Junior cried on the phone and I'd never heard him cry. I closed the toilet seat and sat on it.

"Hey it's going to be ok Junior."

DEVIN

I was excited for several reasons, the main one being that I was about to be a father again. The ability and blessing of bringing a child into this world was such a blessing. I loved my daughter, and would be honored if she had a baby sister, even though a part of me wished for a son of my own. It was going to be a blessing no matter what gender we had. I had many things on my mind while in the elevator, and once the elevator opened I took a deep breath and cleared my thoughts. It was time to explore.

I walked out of the elevator and there was a guy in the hall with a standing desk in front of him. People were walking past him so I tried to do the same thing, but he stopped me.

"Hey let me see your ID." He said.

I reached in my left pocket to grab it, and realized that I didn't' even have my wallet on me.

"I'm about to go back upstairs to get it." I said it with an exaggerated voice, hoping he would see that I didn't feel like going way back upstairs and coming back down, but he didn't give a fuck, he stopped another person and asked them for their ID as well.

I turned and went back to the elevator. As I waited on the

elevator to come down, I started to get exhausted. I understood my wife feeling exhausted because not only did she take the same trip I took, but she was pregnant also. By the time I got in the elevator and got back up to the floor where my room was, I'd come up with a change of plans. Instead of exploring Vegas, instead I was going to just get some rest beside my wife so we could be rested on the same level for when it was time for us to explore together.

I opened the door and shut it, and walked through the living room and down the hall to the bedroom. My wallet was on the nightstand by the bed, so I picked it up and put it in my pocket. I saw the light on in the bathroom, so I knew that's where my wife was. I lay back on the bed and waited on her to come out.

After waiting for about 5 minutes, I heard laughter coming out of the bathroom. It wasn't the type of laughter of if she was watching a comedy special, but the type of laughter that I'd only heard whenever I gave her too many compliments. I swallowed. My heart tumbled around in its container with the curse of anxiety. I loved my wife and I knew she knew that. I told her that all the time and made sure not to miss any opportunities to express to her how I felt. I took deep breaths until I was feeling better, but after 10 more minutes had passed and she still hadn't come out of the bathroom, I started to get concerned.

It wasn't like her to talk in the bathroom anyways. Any time she'd talked on her cellphone, she had that conversation even if she was laying against my chest. To her credit though, maybe she was using the bathroom and the phone rang. I got out the bed because whenever my anxiety was stirred up, I knew there would be sleep no time soon even if it was stirred by a false alarm.

My plan was to go in the bathroom, kiss my wife and tell her I was coming to get my wallet.

I opened the door, and saw that she was on FaceTime with some guy I'd never seen before.

Panic. Fear. Anger. Rage. Calm... I had no reason to feel anything but calm. She hadn't done anything to show me otherwise. We still had our respect.

Ashlon dropped the phone when she saw me.

"Devin you scared the shit out of me."

I stared at her as she reached down to pick her phone up. I couldn't see the screen anymore because the screen was shattered. Somehow, she found a way to hang the phone up, which was the ultimate red flag.

"I don't understand why you just hung up without saying bye..." I was growing more furious by the second.

Ashlon put the phone face down on the sink's counter.

"Yea because I'm wrong Devin. I'm wrong for a few things actually. I should have told you that Ayeeka's father had contacted me recently asking to see his daughter. However, I was only trying to cheer him up because Ayeeka's grandmother died. I should have told you first, but it was such a small situation that I figured you had bigger and better things to deal with."

Ashlon could do no wrong in my eyes. I loved her unconditionally and far greater than anything that I'd ever loved in my lifetime. She was such an impeccable woman, one that I was proud to call my wife.

"Call him back." I said.

She frowned at me. The first time I'd ever seen her frown at me the entire time I'd been with her. "For what?"

"Because I wanna talk to him."

"And say what? Devin he just lost his mother, let him grieve."

She defended his emotions to me, her husband. One thing that I could never tolerate was another woman defending another man who wasn't her father, brother, or husband. She stood in front of me and defended this nigga to me and it had my blood boiling so hard that I was afraid it was going to evaporate.

"You standing here talking about he lost his mother let him grieve. Where was his mother and where the fuck was he when you were sleeping in the cold rain outside of a McDonald's?"

"You throwing that up in my face?" She was combative.

"I'm throwing you a reminder."

"You think I don't remember that I had to be fuckin saved?

You regret saving me or something? You think I forgot that I was a fuckin nobody? Would you rather have a woman who already had it together? Am I not good enough for you anymore?"

"I'm just tryna show you the difference between a nigga who comes around once you make the Forbes list verse a nigga who came around when you didn't have shit or a pot to shit in! That's it that's all!"

"The fuck. You didn't have shit or a pot to shit in either. If anything, we helped each other, don't forget!"

Her words sounded deadly. My zodiac sign plus hers equaled death. A Taurus and a Taurus– two of the kindest, stubbornest combinations ever assembled. Her words in contact against mine were flammable and combustible.

"Before you get to talking about shit that got nothing to do with this conversation, I'ma need you to address why you're defending a nigga who DON'T GIVE A FUCK ABOUT YOU."

Me raising my voice was something I didn't do. Her lips trembled with anger. She was so focused on winning the argument that she wasn't looking at the reason for the argument.

"If we're going to go there, then you can tell me why you're giving all this money and opportunity to a nigga who DON'T GIVE A FUCK ABOUT YOU DEVIN!"

"What? What are *you* talking about?"

"I'm talking about your daddy!"

"Wow. Amazing."

"Amazing is right. Wow is absolutely correct. You coming at my throat all because I'm telling you my daughter's father lost his mother? I guess you wouldn't understand the unspoken bond because you and your baby mama hate without forgiveness."

I wasn't about to continue arguing with her. It was what it was. I turned and left out of the room.

"So you're through talking now?"

I kept walking towards the door, I wasn't interested in anything she was saying. A part of me knew that she knew she was wrong, and didn't know how to express her wrongness in the moment.

There were many men and women who didn't know how to concede when they were dead wrong, and I understood that the anger wasn't directed at me for feeling the way I felt, but it was really self-disappointment that didn't know how to be communicated properly.

"Devin!" She yelled.

I checked my pocket to see if I had the room key, and once I saw that I had it, I put it back in my pocket and reached for the door– she slammed it shut.

You can understand plenty about a person by studying the tendencies of their zodiac signs. I'm a Taurus, whose symbol is a bull. If you think about the characteristics of a bull– one of the most stubborn animals in existence, then you'd spot a flaw that would only be an error when others are involved. Imagine you're a bull... an animal...

Imagine you'd like to do nothing more but stand in one spot all day. Imagine your owner trying to get you to move, yet you haven't the slightest desire to do so. Then imagine the owner trying to do everything possible to get you to move, and nothing ever works. Then imagine one day, your owner walks by you with a red shirt on, and you chase him to no end. Imagine your owner realizing that you hate the color red, and making an event out of it.

Bullfighting.

I was being taunted, and Ashlon was my owner.

"Get out my face Ashlon." I was calm, but she could see the horns in advance. I wasn't to be played with when I was angry, and I knew she knew that.

For a moment I wondered if we would still be together after whatever her next action was going to be. If she pushed me over the edge, there's no telling what was going to happen, no matter how much we loved each other. We both were hurt, and both had different reasons; both of us believing that our individual pain was greater than the others, and both trying to find ways to make a case of pain competing.

She took a deep breath and stepped back.

"I love you Devin. I made a mistake."

I stared at her without replying. My hurt was greater than my ego, and my reaction to anything was going to fall into the pecking order of my genetic makeup. Hurt first, ego second. Two separate mental battles for the same problem. I had to first get over the hurt just to even make it to the fight with the ego. The process of that began with silence.

I walked out and back down to the casino. I had a little over $3,000 in my pocket that night. It's the amount I said I was willing to lose, and no more. I was about to see what the casino had in store for me.

OG TERRANCE

Three shots of Remy had Barbee buzzing. After we lost a few hundred dollars on the slot machines and blackjack tables, we just weren't into gambling as much as we thought we would. The waiters just kept making sure we had free alcohol in exchange for tips, and next thing I knew, we were outside of the casino kissing, not giving a fuck about where we were or who was watching.

She got drunk before me, but it was usually the person who got drunk first who got sober first; so when I got drunk, she was laughing at me and I felt like I'd gotten drunk alone. The alcohol gave Barbee a decent buzz, but since she was accustomed to using hard drugs, her buzz didn't last as long as I was sure mine was going to last. We were taking a walk down Las Vegas strip, hand in hand enjoying the atmosphere and energy. The city was so full of life that it gave us energy that we definitely didn't have initially.

There were all types of hustlers in Las Vegas. There were some who were talented and were able to do magic right in front of your eyes on the streets, there were some artists who could draw a cartoon version of you in 5 minutes– there were models standing around charging money in exchange for pictures, there were even Elvis impersonators complete with the outfit and voice. Everyone was trying to get that next dollar, and had no shame in what they were willing to do in order to make that next dollar a reality.

"Would you like to donate to help fund our basketball team?" A young black guy asked with a folder in his hand.

"Sure." I reached in my pocket to get some money and Barbee stopped me.

"Little boy be gone."

I was offended that she was talking to him like that because all the guy did was ask for help. When he walked away I looked at her with my forehead squinted up.

"Why'd you do that? I was going to help him. At least he's trying."

"Trying to do what?"

"Hell... trying to do the right thing in life."

"That's what you think? You got a lot to learn. Let me show you something." She spoke loud so the boy could hear her. "Aye, come here!"

I pulled the $20 bill out because I was going to give it to him regardless of what she was talking about. I didn't see no harm in helping a young kid. I wished I could have been around to help my son instead of me being in jail all those years. I looked at the guy's outfit as he got closer. He had on tight jeans, the type that I wouldn't' get caught dead in, and I don't care how much in style they were.

"You got some green?"

"How much you want?"

"You got a zip? What about some pills?"

"Shit that can be arranged too. What kind you need?"

◈

In life we should always be careful of who we allow into our life. When we meet a person, we're not just meeting a human with a face and personality, we're also meeting an unpredictable assortment of accumulated spirits.

Sometimes we'll know a person is bad for us— absolutely toxic, and still tell ourselves that we'll be the ones to help and change this person. Many times the attempt to change somebody else, ends up changing us. Sometimes that change is for the better, but sometimes it's for the worse. Trials and tribulations are the variables that add up to life.

I don't even know how it happened.

I only remembered trying to give the guy $20 to donate to his basketball team.

I was standing outside of Caesar's Palace when that happened, but I woke up in the bed and I didn't know what time it was. I felt woozy, and my memory was blurred. Barbee was laying next to me, and we were both naked. I shook her to wake her up, but she didn't wake up. I shook her harder.

"Barbee!"

She still didn't move, so I looked closer to see if she was breathing. When I saw that she still was, I shook her harder, as panic began to creep in my mind.

"Aye!"

"Huh? What?" She jumped up out of whatever hell-hold had its grips on her life.

"Barbee what happened?" I jumped straight to the point.

"Uhm. When?"

"Now! Last night! What happened? You were talking to some boy and now we're waking up?"

"What? Hell nawl. We popped pills, but you was fucked up after one of the ecstasy pills, I think he had a bad batch."

"X-pills? What? What the fuck happened?"

"Nothing... We took the pills, shit... You said let's get a limo... You were horny so we came to the room, but when we got here you took off your clothes, stroked your dick and fell asleep."

My heart was beating fast as hell. I just didn't understand. How the hell did I get so drunk that I didn't even remember taking a pill? I could have had all types of shit done to me last night and I wouldn't have been able to defend anything. That was dangerous, and something that I was never going to do again. I didn't like that at all. I was too old for mistakes like that.

I made an effort to get up and collapsed with a lack of energy. Even though I had a lack of energy, for some reason I couldn't get my mind to stop moving. I needed to just go to sleep and wake back up, but going to sleep seemed like the most difficult task ever. It was weird what that pill had done to me. It made me tired and energetic at the same time. Tired externally, energetic internally.

"What the fuck did he give me for it to be this bad?" I asked as I tried to gain the energy to lift up off of the bed.

When she didn't reply I looked to see what she was doing, and she was sleeping again just that quick. I shook her.

"Aye! What the fuck do you think was in the pill?"

She opened her eyes, and she stared at me but they were glossy.

"Barbee. I asked you a question. What do you think were in the pills?"

She stared at me and started snoring with her eyes wide open.

Exhaustion pressed against my chest and made my breathing difficult. My body was lazy and my mind was racing, and it was scaring me. I tried to reach for the phone, and even though it was close to me, it took so much energy that I didn't think I was going to be able to complete the task. I was about to call my son, but when I read his text messages, I knew I couldn't disappoint him by telling him the situation I was in. I was supposed to be keeping Barbee on the straight path, so if he knew that both of us was fucked up, he might have fired me.

Pops, did y'all book the studio time like I asked you? I told you the PR lady is waiting on me to send her a new Black Barbee track so we can make the announcement. Where the hell y'all at anyways? I'm about to come see y'all.

Barbee started snoring louder, and every exhale let out a trickle of drool that was accumulating on her face. She was such a beautiful woman, but that drool was so disgusting that I couldn't bear to look at her anymore that night. My mind was buzzing, but I didn't know if it was from the alcohol or the pills. Whatever it was a result of, I was praying to come down from my high as soon as possible. I had never in my life been high that long. I sat the phone down on the bed, I didn't have energy to put it back on the nightstand. I closed my eyes praying for sleep to come the way it came for Barbee. I was supposed to be out enjoying Las Vegas, but instead I was stuck. Just as I closed my eyes, another text message came through.

Terrance I was praying and had you on my mind tonight. I haven't heard from you so I hope all is well. I don't wanna pressure you or make it seem like I'm forcing you, but it would really be an honor if you would join our church.

For some reason, when she sent that text to me it angered me. I didn't know why it angered me because it was an act of a kind gesture... She'd been nothing but nice to me and yet here I was seething inside. This wasn't childhood, we were grown adults so I didn't need her to keep telling me that every day. I decided to reply.

When I'm ready to join a church I'll decided which church I wanna join. You don't gotta tell me that every damn day. What's wrong with you? Calm down. Isn't it late anyways? Go to sleep.

I imagined that she would read it and either not respond or get angry. I wasn't about to spare her feelings in regards for her church, and I wasn't obligated to join hers and she needed to know that.

I understand Terrance. I really don't mean to keep saying that every time I text you... Let me come clean with you. A prophet told me that I was going to marry a man from my past. He told me that the man would have a choice between life or death, and that I would have something to do with his choice; and that I was going to be his wife. Then I ran into you, and I kept thinking... Is he my husband God? I know this may be silly to you, but this is one of the reasons I want you to join my church. I'm sorry if this comes across as selfish, but I don't mean for it to be. The other reason I want you to join is because I genuinely think you'll benefit from it. It's not your typical church and the pastor is really talented.

She sent me a super long text, and it was irritating me to read it. What would make her think I would choose her over Barbee? Absolutely not happening.

I'm in a relationship... But I hope you do find what you're looking for. Have a good night.

I tossed the phone down and closed my eyes again, making another attempt at sleep. It worked out that time.

DEVIN

I was staring at my phone as I walked through the casino. I was more interested in what was going on with social media than what was going on with the rest of the world. I was scrolling and switching from Instagram and Twitter, checking out people's opinions of what happened to Drum Killer. The general consensus seemed to be that he had it coming to him. I was still hot about the conversation I'd had with my wife, but I wasn't going to let that ruin my trip. I loved her to no end, so I was sure that we would be fine eventually.

I can't fault her for being on FaceTime with her daughter's father if that's what she felt she needed to do, it was what it was. It kind of caught me off guard though, and I think that was the root of my reaction. Anything is a problem when you're not prepared for it or expecting it. Besides... if her only sin was the fact that she liked to FaceTime her child's father, she was an absolute saint compared to me. I had the nicest side in the world to me, and simultaneously the darkest side a man could possibly possess.

I didn't know how to control my anger.

This was an ongoing issue with me. If you angered me too bad or took something too far, I didn't understand the notion of letting it go. I only understood that I was supposed to have you killed. As a man who went to church regularly– as a man who prayed constantly, it was a living contradiction for me to feel that way. I knew God was a forgiving God, and I knew I was supposed to pray for my enemies and let go. I knew a lot of things I was doing was wrong when it came to channeling anger, but nobody had ever tried to help me correct it. Instead, everyone was trying to help make it worse by carrying out these jobs whenever I got mad. I was getting older, however, and I knew if I wanted to have a chance to raise my kids that I was going to have to change.

"Hey sir. Don't I know you?" An Italian guy wearing a brown and tan colored Caesar's Palace outfit spoke to me from behind a table.

I looked at him as I walked by and shook my head. "Nah." I kept walking but that didn't stop him from being persistent.

"That's fucked up what happened to Drum Killer." He said louder. His words were sharp and matter of fact, and it made me stop and look at him.

"Yea, it is fucked up." I said as I stood there for a moment trying to see what his point was.

"I love your music Q Mack." He said with a huge grin on his face. "I got all of your stuff man, but when you dropped that *Broken Crayons Still Color* song, man that song took the world by storm. I'm fuckin with that. I know I've played that song once a day at least for the last 12 months straight."

I always made time for my supporters when I was able to, and this time wasn't going to be an exception. A supporter of my sounds was the reason I was able to sleep sound at night. I was thankful.

"Thank you." I said smiling.

"Nah, thank you man. Your words got me through some dark times. I appreciate it. Aye... So what brings you to Vegas?"

I'd gotten closer to the table at that point, fully engaged in the conversation; but had I known what lie ahead of me, I would never have stopped at that fuckin table. That conversation was the most expensive one I'd ever had in my life.

Many points of our life are life-changing, and although we stay on the look out for these moments, we could never predict which moments were going to be the heaviest. If you could rewind time and think about the major events that affected your life one way or the other... chances are, you could never see them coming. However, if you saw them coming and you still let it hit you... Then that's a person who believed they were stronger than life. For people who've never had anything bad happen to them, this was a constant lesson in reality.

THE KALEIDOSCOPE

"I just came to Vegas on a quick family vacay. I'd never really done anything in Sin City except perform at shows and concerts. It was really my Dad's idea and I agreed with it."

"Oh word. That's what's up. Vegas is a great place man. You still get down?" He spoke in a lower voice than normal.

"Huh?"

"Smoke? You still smoke? You know weed is legal here."

"Oh. Yea, well... not really, I kinda let all that go ya' know?"

"Word. You don't do nothing? I get down myself, I get high. This is the city for that. Everybody get high here, it don't matter what you do in life. This is the place you can come get high and never get judged. Why you think so many people come here? This is the land of free feels. You gamble?"

I was listening to him, but I knew I was stronger than all of the suggestions he was giving to me. I wasn't about to do any drugs knowing all of the shit I'd gone through. Fuck that. I wouldn't let him get me like that. I chose to reply to his last question however.

"Nah I don't gamble."

"You ever tried?"

"Not really."

"Shit... The kinda money you got, you can get way richer in a casino. It takes money to make money, and if you got it you'll get it forever. It was a guy here last week... he came in here with $100,000. He was a doctor. He made like $300,000 that morning and left to get something to eat. He came back that evening and made another $500,000. He made almost a million dollars in one day."

A million in a day? What? I made a lot of money, but I didn't have any opportunities that was making me a million in a day. I had to sign contracts to record labels to make that kind of money, and the contracts were few in between. A million in a day was unheard of.

"What the hell did he do to make a million?"

"He did all kinds of things. He played some roulette, some craps, some cards. He made a little from each game and left out."

I swallowed. My anxiety was getting the best of me. Hell I was in the mood to make a million right then. "Well how do I play this game? What's this one?"

"This is roulette. All it is... You see the numbers on the board? It's 1 through 36, and two zeros. So it's 38 options... All you do is take a chip and put it on the number you think is going to hit. Then I'm going to take this white ball and spin it around on the inside of this cylinder. If this ball lands on a number that you have picked, you win 35 times whatever you put down."

"Huh? So... If I pick 17 and you hit 17... If I put down $1,000 I'll win $35,000?"

"Hell yea. But I recommend you start with chips that are valued at $5 each so you can get the hang of it."

My mind was racing. "How do I get the chips?"

"Just put your money on the table and I'll exchange them for chips. Once you're done, you can take the chips to the cage and they'll give you cash based on how many chips you have."

I reached in my pocket and pulled out a thousand dollars. I was ready yesterday, even though I didn't know what the hell was really going on. He gave me ten rows of chips, each row worth $100 each and stared at me.

"Now what?"

"Put your chips down on whatever numbers you like and I'm going to spin it."

I put one five-dollar chip down on each of the four numbers I had in mind– 4, 12, 17, and 32. He looked at me with a smirk on my face that I'll never forget. He waited for a second, then picked the ball up and rolled it around the cylinder. I watched as the ball bounced of of the metal ridges from number to number until it finally landed.

"32! You won!" He said as he took a clear shot glass and laid it on top of my chip. "High-five!" He put his hand up, but I wasn't excited yet. What was I to be excited about?

"How much did I win?" I asked.

"$175."

"Wait what? Already?"

"Yea! Just like that!"

I took a second look at the damn game. I hadn't been there but a couple minutes and I was up $175? So at that pace, I could really be up if I focused and went harder. I watched as he counted out $175 worth of chips and slid them over to me. He lifted the glass up and he was ready for me to bet again. This time I doubled my chips up on each number.

"How many numbers can I bet on?" I asked.

"As many as you want to!"

I don't know why he told me that. I damn near covered the board in chips because I didn't wanna lose. Whatever number he was going to hit, I was trying to have. At the last minute, I put a pile of chips on number 20. I don't know why, I don't even know how many chips I'd put down, hell I just did it.

He rolled the ball around the cylinder again, and he was yelled out. "Yea! You got it! 20!"

My mind was racing trying to add up how much money I'd won. I was counting, but I lost track in the midst of the excitement.

"Wow!" A white girl who was playing roulette at another table stepped away from hers to admire my win. "You just killed them. Wow."

I didn't even know how serious it was until a pit boss came over in a suit and started counting how many chips I'd put down on the number. A few people walked over and gave me high-fives. High-fives seemed to be the universal Las Vegas casino language because it's how everybody communicated.

"That's 13 chips on number 20, which is $65. $65 on number 20 brings you $2,275."

My eyes bulged out as I watched him count my racks up. I'd made almost $2,500 just by coming downstairs. If I kept that up, I could leave with a million dollars too. A waitress came by holding a tray in her left hand and a pen in her right hand. She was stunning.

"Hey baby. Congratulations on the win. Can I bring you a drink?"

"Thanks, but no I don't drink."

"Alright baby. Continued luck to you."

It was something about the way she said that... A bitterness, as if she was really wishing me bad luck because I didn't order anything. She walked away and I kept gambling. Before I knew it I had a whole crowd of people watching me beat the casino. I didn't even know how much money I'd made until I got tired of playing. My mouth was dry, and I was tired of talking to all those strangers. Some of them knew who I was and I found myself taking pictures while gambling, which made me even more tired.

It was time for me to get back to the room and see how my wife was doing. I had to tell her about my winning streak. I'd had so much fun I wondered if she wanted to experience it as well.

"I'm done sir." I said as I started looking for a bag to put all of my chips in.

"Alright, well let me give you larger denominations so you can carry them to the cage." He started pulling my chips to him and counting them up. I was trying to guess how much money I'd made, but I had no idea at all.

The white girl who had been playing roulette at the other table was at my table. "You're so lucky. And handsome. I bet all the ladies are after you."

I stared at her without replying. I just wanted this man to count my money up. She was sitting right beside me smiling like it was her who'd won the money and not me. I had my hand on the table while watching the man count my chips, and she placed hers on top of mine. I frowned at her.

"What's up?"

"I like you..."

"I'm married."

"I'm married too."

"Good for you."

"Playing hard to get? Well my room number is easy to remember. It's room 5000. If you ever wanna talk or kick it... Or get high or whatever... Me and my girlfriends are here from Los Angeles and we'd love to kick it with you."

"I'm married."

"I heard you." She walked off without further comment. There was nothing in me, absolutely no urge at all that made me wanna entertain anything she was talking about. I'd been down that road in the past, and there was no urgency to return. All that shit was a child's game. I'd had so many women in my past that there was no certain thrill I was seeking at that point of my life other than a continuously cohesive relationship with the woman that I called my wife.

The dealer slid me two piles of chips. "All yours! $39,470."

My heart skipped a beat. "What? 39 racks?" It was like I was in the twilight zone. I really couldn't believe I'd sat at a table, took $1,000 and turned it to $39,000 in about 90 minutes. That was so crazy to me. I took $1,470 of the chips and handed it to the dealer.

"What?"

"That's a tip."

"Oh shit! Damn I appreciate it man. You're so generous!"

I took the other $38,000 in chips and marched my generous ass straight to the cashier. Shit if he thought I was generous; his ass was just sweet! He gave me $38,000 when I was just minding my damn business sulking in my misery. I slid my chips across the counter and expected them to give me some type of cashier's check or money order. She left my chips on the counter top and walked to the back room. She came back out of the back room with a manager and a huge pile of hundred dollar bills in her hands. The manager re-counted the chips and nodded her head.

I watched as the first lady dropped a stack of hundreds in a money machine and pressed the button. She clipped it and dropped another one, clipped that one and dropped another one— then she wrapped it in three $10,000 bundles, $5,000 bundles, and $3,000 in loose hundreds. She made one pile and slid it all across the counter to me just like that. No questions, nothing.

I picked the money up and stuffed it in all of my pockets. I'd only brought $3,000 to gamble with, but I was up so much that I decided to go buy gifts for my wife. It was a mall inside of Caesar's Palace, and I was going to grab her some new Versace purses— I saw some back when I was in Atlanta but I knew I had a few expenses that needed to be paid before I grabbed those purses. They were $2,000 each, and I definitely had to buy her a pair of shoes for each purse. That's like an $8,000 ticket plus tax. That was nothing though when I could make almost $40k in less than two hours.

The shopping mall was open 24 hours during the busiest month of Las Vegas, so I went shopping immediately. I bought her purses, shoes, then went to get me some new shoes also. I was about to get me four pair of Giusseppes, which was going to come up to around $6,000. All that, plus I had cash to blow. My trip was going amazing and it was just getting started.

OG TERRANCE

It was a little around 8 in the morning when I finally got the energy to get up out of the bed. 8 AM Las Vegas time was the equivalent of 11 AM Atlanta time, so I knew something was wrong because I never slept that late. I couldn't even recall what happened the night before, but I did know that I felt sick to my stomach. I didn't feel hungry, it felt if you held your breath wanting to take a deep breath and hadn't yet. My stomach, my body, it all felt clogged up.
"Barbee." I said groggily, but just speaking made me weaker.
She opened her eyes and squinted. "Oh I feel so sick. Ugh." She closed her eyes back and rolled over. "Man we slept the whole night."
"I know. Q Mack want us to get in the studio... He needs some songs asap... Like this morning so we gotta get out of this slump."
"What? Ok. Well... I gotta take something... I can't do a song feeling like this... I gotta be high to record this early... As sick as I am..."
"Well... Weed is legal here, so..."
"Nah, I got something." She opened the drawer up and pulled out the pouch that she told me she was keeping her money in. It

wasn't money she pulled out, but a tiny tube with pieces of small butter colored rocks inside.

Crack.

"Where the fuck you get that from?"

"From the nigga who asked us to donate to his basketball team."

I placed my face in my palm. This woman was too damn fine to be a crackhead. This shit was crazy. I shook my head and stared at her like she'd lost her mind.

"What?"

"Man flush that shit."

"You want me to record the songs or what?"

"So you can't record sober? You ain't got no talent or something? You want me to write your damn songs?"

She frowned at me. "Don't act like you like me just because of the way I look. I'm different, I have problems, and this is how I solve them."

I looked away and sighed. I really didn't know what to say to that.

"Hey... Terrance it's just temporary. I'm quitting this shit as soon as I can get this mixtape recorded. Just work with me please..."

"Man I can't condone—"

"Well I can't record. Tell Q Mack I'm out of the deal. I don't wanna be under this pressure. I just wanna live my life and be happy the way I was. I didn't ask you to sign me, you asked me to sign with ya'll."

"But you signed the contract already and took the money. I can't—"

"Fuck that money. He can have it back, I'd rather take my freedom and just go smoke and be happy doing my lil shows."

"Man just smoke the shit so we can hit the studio."

She smiled as soon as I got the words out, and as soon as she started putting her stuff together, my phone rang. When I glanced at the caller ID, I knew I had to take that call because I'd been busy the last few times he called; and he definitely deserved better treatment after all he'd done for me. I excused myself, got up and started walking towards the door.

"Hello." The deep voice vibrated in my ear.

"Hey Banny! My main man, what's up?" I owed this man everything for helping me get my son out. He was a friend for life, and I would do whatever for him.

"A few things are up Terrance..." He sounded disappointed but I didn't know why. "I've been trying to reach you for a few months now."

I exhaled. Although I would do anything for him, life had a way of interrupting and slowing you down even though that's not your intention.

"I'm sorry Banny. I've been helping my son run the record label and stuff ya' know. It's been taking a toll–"

"Nigga what the fuck are you doing free?" His deep voice boomed with anger.

"What do you mean why am I free? You mean why am I free out of prison?"

"Nigga you know what the fuck I'm saying. How the *fuck* did you get free?"

"You know how I got free... My son's wife got me a lawyer..."

"I gave you that information for your *son* to get out nigga, not your old ass. You out here running around like you some type of big shot celebrity and shit, but you took my kindness for weakness!"

I frowned. I didn't understand why he was talking to me the way he was, we'd been friends for decades. We'd never had an argument and never been on opposing ends of a power struggle.

"You gave me the info for my son and it worked, but the info was so good that they decided to let me go too. I don't understand... Are you jealous or something?"

"Nigga you a fuckin snitch basically. You don't think I could have used the shit to get out my damn self? But nah, I gave it to you to help you out. I did you a solid, but you shit on me by using it for yourself too? Then you think you doing something all in pictures on TMZ with that young rappin bitch? Nigga don't forget you a old head, and you are subject to old head rules."

I didn't have the patience to continue arguing with him. He was clearly angry, and I wasn't about to entertain that. I was free, and he was locked up— common sense would have told him that I would have been way more beneficial to him as a friend instead of an enemy. He was just going to have to learn the hard way.

"I never shitted on you Banny, I always respected you. But I guess you're mad. I guess you woke up in that shitty ass prison cell and got mad that I decided to come be a productive member of society. So with that being said... Good luck and I wish you well friend."

"Nigga I dare you to—"

Click. I double tapped the end button on my cell phone and blocked his number. I had no reason to contact him and he had no reason to contact me either. He'll be fine, fuck that... at least I tried.

I was about to send Devin a text, but I decided to check social media first so he wouldn't be angry. Instagram still had a lot of RIP posts about that Drum Killer nigga, and a lot of his fans were reacting on the internet talking about senseless violence. I kept scrolling and saw a post on one of the smaller blogs talking about Drum Killer had surveillance footage at the house. I laughed because that blog always came up with lies and fake rumors in order to get followers and website traffic. The only reason I followed it was because the shit they came up with for my son was funny sometimes.

I scrolled further and I saw another blog sharing that story also. I kept scrolling and another blog was reporting about the surveillance footage. I went to TMZ to see what they were talking about, and there it was in bold letters.

WE ARE WORKING TO ACQUIRE THE SURVEILLANCE FOOTAGE OF A MAN LEAVING DRUM KILLER'S PROPERTY AFTER HIS MURDER. STAY TUNED

AND SUBSCRIBE TO SEE THE VIDEO THE MOMENT WE POST IT.

If felt like the floor had been pulled from underneath me. How good was this footage? What did it show? How long was it? What about the clarity? Would people know that it's me or would it just look like someone who could be me? I had several questions worked out mentally prior to me seeing this video. I was pissed and anxiety was starting to get the best of me.

I went to the biggest blog, The Shade Room to see if they were reporting it, and they had an entirely different story going on. I shook my head as I wondered if the world was trying to attack me and my family for fun.

PRODUCER SUES Q MACK AND PRODUCER FOR ALLEGEDLY STEALING THE INSTRUMENTAL TO BIGGEST HIT SONG, BROKEN CRAYONS STILL COLOR.

The spotlight was always brighter than the blind spots. If the school teachers and educators had to add three special courses to the curriculum, I would recommend that they add law, money, and fame. These were the missing lessons that seems to round out the biggest flaws of humanity. Learning about how hot the Earth's core was seemed to never compare to learning how hot you could make a judge by going to trial. Remembering how to simplify fractions had nothing on simplifying who you allowed into your circle. I took a deep breath.

DEVIN

Last night turned out to be the best night I'd had in a long time. Ashlon had been brought to tears when I showered her with the gifts, and she'd apologized for her actions. I felt bad for overreacting when it wasn't even that serious. I don't know why I was even tripping though, because I knew my wife if I didn't know anything else. She was a real one, and I knew that she only had my best interests at heart even if she made a mistake and didn't have them at mind.

We made love well into the morning, make-up sex– Making up for any shortcomings with long comings.

Everything was wonderful. Me and Ashlon went to sleep with our bodies intertwined, and we woke up the same way. She woke up first of course, because I'd had less rest.

"Babe. Your phone is going off."

I heard my wife's gentle voice and felt a gentle shake. "Babe wake up. Your phone has been ringing for five minutes."

I woke up with my eyes still closed. I reached for the phone and had trouble grabbing it but Ashlon placed it in my hand. I knew I needed to get it together and get out of my sleepiness. When I remembered that I was in Las Vegas and had a new way to make money, I woke all the way up. The happiness I felt from having a new hustle was unexplainable. Life was good.

"Answer the phone babe. They've been calling you nonstop."

I pulled my body up and leaned against two propped up pillows. I exhaled when I saw my lawyer's name on the caller ID.

"Yo."

"Devin. Really?"

"What? What did I do?" My wife took a deep breath as she braced herself for whatever news she knew I would eventually tell her.

"Drum Killer. Please tell me you didn't have anything to do with this Devin."

I hurriedly turned the volume down on the phone before replying. The new iPhones are loud, so I'm sure she heard some of what he said if not all. "What are you talking about? How dare you accuse me of something like that? I should fire you!"

"Wait... Wait... I'm sorry. That wasn't very professional of me. However, I did just get a call from a very good friend of mine who works at the police station. He says they have surveillance footage but haven't released the details yet to the public."

My heart sank and my mouth dropped open as I braced myself for the worst news I could possibly hear. I should have known my pops didn't know what the fuck he was doing. If anything, I should have just done it myself if I was still going to get the same amount of time for the shit.

"What's wrong baby?" My wife's soft voice interrupted the harshness of the dilemma.

I got out of the bed, tossed on a shirt and slid my feet into my shoes. I walked outside to finish the conversation. As I was trying to close the door, my wife was standing there. My mind was so gone I didn't even know she'd followed me to the door.

"Babe... let me handle this real quick. I'll be right back."

She took a deep breath and shook her head. I hated to feel like I was letting her down in any capacity... I made a mental note to spend some time with her for the rest of the day to get her mind off of any worrying. I checked to make sure I had my room key, and I closed the door.

"Pete what the fuck. Did he say what was on the surveillance tape?" I was on the verge of a complete meltdown, all thanks to my Dad. His mistake was a costly one, and I hated that I was going to have to be the person who paid for it.

"Yea he said what was on the tape."

I exhaled. "Fuck man. This shit is crazy. I don't know what to do Pete. Man I just–"

"It's a million dollar Easter egg if you want him to hide it."

My lawyers voice was crisp, sharp, arrogant, defiant. It was the tone of a person who knew how to execute a flawless victory, no matter what lengths or who had to be destroyed in order to achieve it. He had me and it was nothing I could do about it.

"A million dollars? Pete really? He's charging me a million dollars to hide it?"

"No sir. I'm charging you a million dollars."

I felt like someone took a knife and literally pierced me without me looking. It was so hurtful knowing the series of events that led to this one. Once my last lawyer quit on me, I was forced to find a new one. Me being so fuckin petty and vengeful... I went and fired the very person that my old lawyer competed with for business. I knew my lawyer hated this guy as a person, and I just wanted to do all I could to be vengeful. I swallowed when I realized that I'd constantly been fighting the one thing I'd known my entire life.

Dearly beloved, avenge not yourselves, but rather give place unto wrath: for it is written, Vengeance is mine; I will repay; saith the Lord.

I was taught this as a kid, and re-taught it in my adolescence, and still couldn't let go of my reactions to anger. I didn't have a million dollars to give, hell that's almost all I had left, despite what the Forbes lists reported to the world. I knew I couldn't tell him I didn't have it because my life was on the line. I knew that if they arrested my Pops that they were going to arrest me too because they already knew that was my M-O.

"Alright Pete. I'll get it to you. Let me get it to you in installments... How about $100,000 a month for 10 months?"

"No sir. A half million up front, and $250,000 a week for the next two weeks. That should give you some time to liquidate anything if you need, but I know you have a half million; so let's make that happen now."

My back was against the wall, but I wasn't going to lose this time. I had a new hustle, so just as smooth as he was trying to finesse me, I was going to finesse that cash right back in my hands.

"Aight Pete. I'll have my accountant wire it to you."

"No sir, you will not. You're going to invest in bitcoin, something you're known for anyways, and then you're going to forward the bitcoin to my crypto wallet. Simple as that. I'll send you my wallet address later."

He was slick. Forwarding bitcoin was under the radar, undetectable. Nobody had to know anything other than I'd made an investment into bitcoin. I took a deep breath and stretched my neck from side to side while thinking about how I was about to recoup from that million-dollar loss. To make up for it I was about to try to make $2 million in the casino. I was going to take that loss and then go drop another million on buying a Burger King restaurant purchase. I was going to show all of them a lesson.

"Alright Pete. No problem."

"Aye... Devin. After you handle that, I'll let you know what we're going to do about that lawsuit the producer just put on you today."

"What? The fuck?" If it wasn't one thing it was another. Fame and riches was a never-ending struggle to keep it or lose it. Anybody who's ever had any sizeable amount of money has had to play tug of war the entire time with it in their possession, and every time the rope tugged one direction or the other, it constantly burned a hole in their own personal peace. I wasn't going to lose the war, nor my peace. I had a plan.

"I'll hit you later Pete."

I hung up and walked back in the room and sat down on the

bed. I picked up the remote and turned to ESPN like nothing was wrong.

"Uhm Devin. Don't try me. What's going on?"

I really didn't wanna talk about it. Again.

"It was just a misunderstanding. It's cleared up now."

"Devin... What's going on?"

"Nothing."

I could see her anger horns starting to grow out of the corner of my eyes. Tension was pressing itself into her beautiful face, and her breathing became shallow and deep.

"It was a rumor going through the blogs or something about me having something to do with the rapper."

"You mean the rapper who got killed."

"Yea, that."

Ashlon grabbed the remote and searched for the mute button. The commentators were talking about if Lebron James was going to either stay in Cleveland or go to a different team. Then there was silence.

"Devin did you have anything to do with that?"

I looked at her like she was crazy. She definitely knew not to ask me anything like that. I wasn't sure what was up with her lately.

"Of course not."

"Devin be honest. The girls told me you had an altercation at the studio. I respected your wishes when you didn't wanna talk about it, but now I'm asking you if you had anything to do with that man's murder?"

"Are you a detective or something? What's up with you?"

"I'm not a detective, I'm a protector. Which means I wanna protect your soul if I can. But if you're not letting me know what's going on, then as your wife then what can I do but stand by while the devil constantly beats at you and tries to trick you."

I was getting mad and she could sense it. "The devil can't trick me again, he doesn't exist in my world. Period."

"I'm just asking if you had anything to do—"

"No!" I lied. "You're no different than the lawyers or the blogs. All y'all think is the worst of a black man. That's a damn shame, and I'm your husband is what makes it even worse." I had all the theatrics while feeling guilty inside. I know they say God forgives, but what about when the person asking for forgiveness is getting out of control? I needed to go to church soon. The feeling I had was as if I'd gotten in trouble in school and my Grandparents were going to find out once I got home. An ominous, nervous vibe.

"I'm sorry Devin. I'm really, truly sorry. I love you ok?"

"I love you too."

She got up and grabbed her phone off of the nightstand. A part of me knew she was about to text or FaceTime that nigga again. I could always spot changes in actions, changes in behavior, and changes in emotion, and even though I'd spotted it, I didn't have time to work on it at the moment because I had work to do. I had to see what the fuck was up with my Pops, and I had to go make $2 million before the vacation was over.

LIKA

I went above and beyond for Brown. I washed his clothes, cooked his dinner, cleaned the house... I did every little thing I could to try to make him happy, even while enduring post partum depression. I knew he loved me and I knew he loved his little boy, but the look on his face was as if I was disgusting to him in ways. Not disgusting sexually, but disgusting because of my inability to contribute the way he wanted me to. He was always comparing our life to Devin's and constantly pushing me to get more out of him.

A part of me felt like he was using me, but he was doing a damn good job at disguising the fact if he was. I was in my thoughts as we both lay on the sofa watching celebrity Family Feud. I was laying against him and he had his arm around me. This episode's guest was Kanye West and Kim Kardashian, and just before Steve Harvey could tell his first joke, Brown interrupted with a question.

"Does your baby daddy know him?"

I got sick of answering questions about that damn man honestly. I thought it would fade by now, but it seems it had only picked up in momentum. It was like he had a private mental fight with trying to compare his value and place in my life to what Devin's was.

"I'm not sure who he knows..."

"You never met Kanye or Kim?"

I exhaled and didn't say anything.

"Hey. Did you hear me?"

"Nah I don't know them baby. I never met them."

There was more silence in the room afterwards. I loved Brown, I really did, and I had great patience with him when I probably would have snapped had it been someone else. The truth was, every person had flaws, and it was just up to us to determine which flaws we were willing to accept in life, and which ones we knew we couldn't deal with. I didn't learn this until long after Devin was gone, but had I known what I knew now....

I brushed that thought away, and grabbed my man's hand with my own.

"I know I can't do for you right now on a major level, but I do try my best Lika. My Instagram ain't poppin, and neither is my Facebook, but my love for you is definitely poppin. If you would, just please be patient with me. I'll get us in a better situation and you'll be able to stop accepting money from that cat."

I sat up because I needed him to understand me clearly. While I respected his desires, I also wanted him to see what my own desires were.

"Brown, that's not important to me. You see... a lot of men think that money is what it takes to keep a woman around, but that's not true. Us women... we get offers from men with more money and power nearly every day of the week. We are women... so we are pursued, we are valuable as the ones who can give a man what another man can not... a life."

We looked at our son simultaneously as he slept in his mini-rocker. Brown swallowed and took a deep breath. He didn't have any words, but I could sense his mind was still wondering, and I wanted to put him at ease.

"Brown I love you. You see that's the thing that makes us

different than men. When a woman loves... truly loves a man, then nothing else matters except the union of the two of them. A woman can't accept mediocrity from a man she doesn't love, but for a man she loves, mediocrity could never exist in her mind; only his."

I felt a tingle go through me as he kissed me on the neck. I loved him, even though I knew there would always be friction based on how close him and Devin were at one point, but I was determined to make it work out for the best. It was also amazing how many questions Brown had when he was supposed to once have been a friend of Devin's, but it just goes to show that you really never know anybody.

OG TERRANCE

Banny had a lot of power in the streets, and not being locked up with him everyday made that memory fade a little when it shouldn't have. After I thought about his words, I found myself looking over my shoulders right and left, as everyone started looking suspicious suddenly. I'd tried to call him back, but he'd blocked my phone number, and I didn't need that type of energy out here. Freedom was taking me longer to get accustomed to than I thought. I thought since I was older that I would be able to get out of prison and live perfect with the knowledge I'd accumulated, but it was the opposite. I was like a newborn in a brand new world with new principles.

The music was a mess.

Although I found her extremely talented, I found myself unable to get into the music that Black Barbee was making while at the studio. Instead, I found more entertainment in looking over my shoulder to make sure that Banny didn't send anybody to kill me. I understood from his perspective what his issue was, but that just didn't make all the sense in the world to me. Why shouldn't I have used the information as leverage in my situation as well? It was strong enough to free both me and my son, and I thought that if a person wanted to help you, they should want the best for you. The phone vibrating startled the fuck out of me.

"Pops where the fuck you at?"

I exhaled. I'd rather my son fuss at me than being locked up letting the correctional officers fuss at me. Fuck that.

"I'm at the studio. She has 3 songs recorded already, and she's working on another one right now. Are you coming by? She asked when you two were going to meet."

"She'll be ok for now. Just keep her recording."

"Aight."

"Pops you really gon act like you don't know what's going on with this Drum Killer situation? I know you've been seeing the rumors on the blogs. What's up with that? If you didn't know what you were doing you shouldn't have fuckin done it."

I hated that I felt like I let him down. I'd made an honest mistake in a world where mistakes got your life snatched away. "All I can do is apologize son. I'd been locked up so long that I wasn't thinking about cameras and surveillance."

"Apparently you weren't thinking about checking for witnesses either. Y'all didn't do that back in y'all day? Or y'all just liked prison that much?"

"I'm sorry son. I fucked up."

"Sorry won't always cut it Pops. And what happens when the shit hits the fan? Tell me what you would do at that point."

I looked at Barbee and she smiled at me from the booth. I loved that lady, and I loved my life, as it was a far cry from the grip of the prison's suffocating containment. I wasn't prepared to go back again. I knew Banny would kill me the moment I walked through the doors if that happened.

"If it came to that, let them crackers do their job."

I heard my son exhale and mumble to himself. That wasn't the answer he wanted to hear, but hell that was a situation I didn't wanna be in either. I'm not about to confess to shit, and I don't care if they had a surveillance footage with my ID and blood sample on the scene. I still wasn't about to make it easy for the cops to hide me forever.

"So basically... it's whatever right?"

I also couldn't afford to lose the support from my son, so I had to play the middle. "It's not whatever. I won't ever let you take a hit like that. I'll handle it to the best of my abilities. You stop worrying about it and let me worry about it. It's going to work out."

Words were rambling off of my tongue before they rattled through my mind. It wasn't easy handling dirt with a microscopic spotlight beaming down on you, but it's what he ordered me to do and I did it to the best of my ability. In my opinion he shouldn't have even been tripping for real. I'd done the shit for free, and never asked him about any type of money. I did it for no other reason than I was his Pops.

"Pops this is costing me greatly... but I still appreciate you for being there for me, even though it wasn't the best execution. Hopefully you're handling the Black Barbee situation better than you handled the Drum Killer assignment."

"I am son. I'm going to send you a few songs in a couple of hours for you to sift through. I think you're going to like the way the songs are coming out."

"I definite hope so Pops. I need to be able to recoup some of that money back as soon as I'm able to. Send me the songs you already have, and the other ones once they're done."

"Aight. I got you. I'm on it."

I hung the phone up and walked back to the table. The engineer was nodding his head to the beat while Barbee rapped about using niggaz to get to where she wanted to get in life. Of course it made me feel some type of way listening to her talk like that, but I also understood that it was just entertainment and nothing personal. My son said plenty of stuff in his songs that I didn't think he really meant.

"Whew! Play that back!" Barbee came out of the booth wide eyed, sweaty, jumpy, and with too much energy. Her blood vessels were protruding from the side of her temple, she looked like she was in the middle of a strenuous workout. She needed to calm down. She grabbed the bag off of the table and started walking to the bathroom.

"Barbee. Wait." I got up to go speak to her privately, the producer and engineer were staring at me like I was crazy for interrupting her while she was in her groove, but I was starting to get concerned. She initially told me she only had to hit the rock one time and she would be fine to do a whole studio session, but it seemed to me that she'd doubled back to that bag 5 times at this point. I didn't need her OD'ing on me again and my son pissed at me again for nothing handling the situation better.

"What's up OG?" She started laughing. It was a laugh that reminded me of Gucci Mane's video when he started laughing about his Bart Simpson chain smoking. A laugh that could only come from a person too far gone.

"Step out, lemme speak to you real quick."

"Step in the bathroom with me and we can speak all you want."

I exhaled and followed her to the bathroom. I really wanted her to quit that nasty habit. It was starting to get out of control at this point, and I was the only person who cared for her to tell her anything different. She was much of a phantom in life. A star with a large following, a beautiful woman with the capacity to be a mega-star in this world, yet quiet and invisible simultaneously, empty inside with all of her emptiness filled with the lightweight accumulation of a large mass of personal problems. An invisible treasure.

I shut the door to the bathroom, and waited a few moments until they started the music back before I started talking.

"So you just gon smoke crack the whole studio session?"

Barbee rolled her eyes, yet continued on about her business like I hadn't said anything.

"You don't care about your health? Your well-being? You don't care about your reputation or your body?"

"Niggaaaaa. What the fuckkkkk."

I couldn't just back down just because she was aggravated. Hell I was just as aggravated.

"You were just in the hospital Barbee. I mean can't you—"

"Nigga... And you were just acting like you wanted to be with me. If you wanted to be with me for real you'd be supporting me instead of acting like my damn father. What the fuck. You my boyfriend or my damn daddy?"

I can't lie and say that her words didn't cut. They were brutal for someone who was already self conscious about the age discrepancy. I was about to be 47 and she was still in her 20s. A part of me still felt like I was still in my 20s also. In my 20s was when I was trapped and kidnapped by the system, who held me until I had no 20s remaining to live out. I was trying to get Barbee not to make the same mistakes I'd made— not listening to people who knew better... but it was a downhill battle. She could have any man she wanted, so if I wanted to be with her I would have to get with the program.

"What does that feel like?" I asked as I stared at her take a deep pull on the pipe.

She held the smoke in for as long as she could and let it all out with a deep moan. Her eyes were blood shot, shifty, her mouth trembling as if she was in the freezing cold.

"Whew!" She yelled out as she took back to back deep breaths. It was as if she had an extra burst of energy, as if she was ready to run a marathon or join a gym right at that moment. They say crack was bad for you, but she looked like she was having the time of her life.

"You wanna try it with me instead of judging me?"

"Oh no."

"Why not? Because you heard bad things about it? Have you ever tried it before?"

"Nah... I haven't."

"Then try it. It's no different than anything else. Besides... If you can handle heroin without tripping out, then I know you can handle crack. This ain't even as bad as the pill you had last night."

Anger began to cover my body like the 7 AM sunrise. I felt deceived, stupid, slow, and naïve. Despite me having years of experience over me, I guess there was no amount of experience that could prepare a person for the surprises of the streets. My breathing increased and she could tell I was pissed.

"Baby... Things are not as bad as people make it seem to be. I just want you to see from your own perspective instead of you judging me just because of what the rest of the world thinks. Fuck what the world thinks... Baby we're in our own world. You took me from out of a bad relationship, and I thank you for that, but why not have some fun while we still have life on this earth?"

I leaned against the wall as I watched her shifting eyes. She was so alert that I don't think anything could get past her even if it tried. I was tired of being on the opposite side of the field with Barbee... I wanted her to like me for me, I didn't want her to see me as someone she couldn't have fun with.

"Aight I'll try it."

She handed me the pipe and held the lighter under the target area. She cracked the flame open and it wasn't long before the smoke was circulating inside of the small brass tube. I took an inhale, and when I tried to hold it as long as she did, I almost threw up letting the smoke back out. That smoke was aggressive, fighting with my lungs and throat, punching my chest with the unforgiving fragrance of a forbidden set of chemicals. The aftertaste was that of Arm and Hammer toothpaste when you hadn't yet rinsed after brushing, and the after-effect was nothing like I'd seen on television or read in any books.

It was like a ghost climbed inside of you and sprinkled Hennessy on my soul, relaxing me on a level I'd never felt before. I suddenly understood how she had so much energy, because I had it as well. I felt as if I could jump over a car, or stay awake for the next week straight with no sleep. I felt an internal tingle that stretched from the inside of my head all the way down to my toes. It was the psychological equivalent of the night before Christmas, except if you pause that moment for the entire duration while under the influence of the powerful drug.

"Wow." I pressed myself up on my calf muscle, and raised myself up and down as if I was at the gym. I could hear my heart beating loud as fuck, the fast pace of it thumping in my ear as if I had a stethoscope. I had so much excess energy that I started jogging in place to the beat of the music.

"Ayee! Ayee! Ayee! Ayee!"

Barbee was chanting to my dance, and I didn't even know it was a dance until I realized that I was doing the same thing I saw a rapper doing when he opened up to one of my son's show. Blocboy JB.

"Aye! Aye! Aye! Aye!" Barbee kept chanting and for the life of me, I swear I couldn't control myself. I opened the door and fell, prompting the engineer and producer to look at me like I was crazy. They saw that Barbee was laughing and chanting and started laughing also, although I'm sure they had no clue what the hell was going on. I jumped up and kept dancing to the beat of Barbee's music. I no longer cared what anybody thought of me, it was like the drug had given my mind permission to fly and be free.

The song went off and I continued dancing. I didn't care.

"Old School... Chill." The producer said as I started jumping closer and closer to his keyboard and drum machine. I heard his voice but my brain didn't process it completely to give my body orders to chill. I just had so much energy. I kept bouncing and jumping up and down, and didn't realize how bad I was sweating until it started burning my eyes. I wiped my eyes and opened them wider, and it was like I was seeing things I'd never seen before. I was able to zoom in on individual strands of hair on people's face, even while jumping up and down.

I stopped jumping, breathing heavily, my throat constricting as if I was swallowing water even though there was nothing in my throat but fear and high blood pressure.

"Terrance. You ok?" I heard an alien speak to me in surround sound. I jumped up and put my hands out like a karate kid. I wasn't about to let the aliens kidnap me. I started looking from right to left like a trapped kitten, and I was going to strike whatever alien touched me first.

"Hi-yah!" I swung my arm to attack whichever one was nearest me, making contact with warm skin. I jumped back and felt my body lift off of the ground. They were kidnapping me and it was nothing I could do. I was floating, soaring, flying—airborne... Then I went slamming down on the ground, rolled and hit my head on the wall.

"Ouch!"

"What the fuck wrong with you nigga?"

I snapped out of my senses, still breathing hard, lost, confused. The producer was standing over me with his fists balled up. "Nigga you hit her in the face you dumb ass old ass nigga. And you almost fucked my equipment up. Get the fuck out of my studio nigga."

Barbee had a busted lip, blood was pouring down her chin and I had no idea how it happened. She wasn't even crying, she was staring at me as if she was concerned.

"Hi-Q, it's ok. Let him make it. It's my fault." Barbee said, defending me. When she took up for me I knew she loved me, and it made me love her even more.

"Don't ever take up for a nigga who hits you Barbee! You're too beautiful for that shit. Y'all fuckin' or something? Y'all wigging the fuck out. I'm not doing no more production today. Y'all get the fuck out."

"Wait." I said. "I'm sorry. I'm truly sorry." I was apologizing, but I couldn't stop that excess energy from making me look like a paranoid kitten.

"Nah, get out now! Ain't shit sorry. I'll send the songs and the bill for the beats to Q Mack, but I don't ever wanna see y'all again. Get the fuck out!"

I got up, and thought I seen the engineer recording us with his phone, but I had no proof— he could have just been making a phone call or reading a text message. I grabbed Barbie's hand, and she grabbed her small bag of goodies and we left the studio. We didn't need them anyways, as long as we had us.

DEVIN

My Pops sent me a text earlier letting me know we had enough songs recorded to release a 7 song mixtape. I was excited about it because I needed all the streams of income I could possibly get. I had lawyers that needed to be paid, bills, too many random investments that hadn't been proven... I was determined to not let my life fall back into the misery that it once was. I focused as I sat at the roulette table with $3,000 worth of chips in front of me. It was a different dealer than the one who'd initially taught me how to play the game. The other dealer was a fan of mine. This one looked like a hater, but it didn't matter. I was about to take the casino for everything, fuck that.

    I put chips straight down the middle of the board, covering my favorite numbers— 2, 5, 7, 8, 11, 14, 17, 20, 23, 26, 29, 32, and 35. There was only 3 columns that the ball could possibly land on, and I had an entire column covered up. By my estimates, that gave me a 33% win probability. With this method, I should be able to win big because I would win once every three times the dealer spun the ball.

    He tossed the ball around the cylinder, and my heart pounded as I watched it land.

"10!" The dealer yelled out. He scraped my chips off of the table and stood there waiting on me to put my chips back down. I felt salty that I didn't win anything, but I knew I had to win at least every three tries. This time I doubled my chips on the same exact numbers, knowing that if I hit this time I would be way up.

"Would you like something to drink?" A waitress interrupted me as I was trying to put my last chips down.

"No more bets." The dealer waved his hand across the table.

"One more number." I said. "Number 32. I was interrupted."

"Sorry, no more bets." The dealer replied.

"Do you want something to drink?" The waitress was annoying me.

I watched in fear as the white ball bounced around the cylinder. There was no way that ball was going to land on the very number that I didn't bet. Not out of all the numbers on the board, I just knew better...

"32!" He said with enthusiasm. I watched in anger as he raked all of my chips off of the table and into a box. "Gotta get your bets in a little sooner!"

The dealer was so nonchalant. He didn't give a fuck about me or the loss I'd just taken. The waitress was still standing there.

"Aye Ms. Lady. Can you get out my face?"

She had the nerve to look offended. "Better luck to you." She said as she walked off.

I didn't care, about people wanting me to lose, because I was a natural born winner. I looked at my pile of chips and noticed that I was down to $1500. I'd lost $500 the first time, $1,000 the second spin, and I was about to put the whole $1500 down to shake back. I placed my bets quickly this time, being sure not to miss any of my favorite numbers.

"No more bets." The dealer rolled the ball around the cylinder at a pace faster than he normally rolled. "Good luck." He said as he looked around the casino like he was bored.

I stood up and stared at the ball as it bounced from number to number. My heart beat faster as the ball bounced slower. It was getting closer and closer to my number. It stopped and landed back on the same exact number, 32. And as soon as I was about to let out a cheer, it popped out and landed in the zero slot.

"Zero!" The dealer racked the last of my chips off of the table and into the casino's box. "Better luck to you." He said to me as if nothing had happened. My blood pressure was high, and I was angry enough to swing on him, but I couldn't let him or the casino see me sweat. Hell I had a million dollars cash in the bank, so I knew I could flip to two million if I caught the right streak. Nobody could lose that many times in a row, at least not me... my luck ain't that damn bad.

"Aye. Where do I go to make a withdrawal?" I paced from one foot to the other and looked around the casino desperately. I wanted to (a) show them that I hadn't lost nothing but chump change, and (b) get my chump change the fuck back.

"You can make a withdrawal at the ATM over there." The dealer pointed in the corner like I was some type of chump.

"They'll let me take out $100,000 at the ATM?" I asked arrogantly.

He looked at me differently when I said that. The look on his face let me know that he'd misjudged me for another poor black nigga just wasting his time in the casino. I relished in the power that the money had over him when he thought he was the one carrying all of the power over me.

"Oh. Well. Do you have a player's card?" He asked, all of a sudden trying to go through casino protocol.

"I don't have one. What is a player's card?"

"One second." The dealer waved his hand and a manager came over. He whispered in the manager's ear, and it was like the entire mood changed.

"Hi sir. My name is Sammy. I'm a casino host here at Caesar's Palace. I understand that you'd like to make a bank withdrawal?"

Sammy whisked me away to an extreme high roller's section on an unlisted floor. When I entered the room, I could tell right away that the entire vibe and experience was about to be way different from where the hater was rolling the roulette ball. There were waitresses walking around, but they had nothing on but body paint. The lighting was dim, but the tables, chips, and cards were all illuminated to make sure you could see what you were doing.

Sammy walked me to a cage so I could make a withdrawal. They handed me a solid gold diamond studded ink pen and a sheet of paper for me to write down how much I wanted to take out of my account.

"Take your time. What's your name again?"

"Devin."

"Yes, Devin. Take your time Devin. Feel free to walk around and move at your own pace." He handed me a celebratory cigar and a black key for me to access that private VIP room whenever I felt like it. He walked away and before I could write something on the paper, I heard a loud series of cheers accommodated with loud clapping.

"Yay! You did it Mikey! Good job! Yay!"

A small crowd came over and patted Mikey on the back as he stood at the dice table with a slight grin on his face. I walked over to the table to take a look. He had the type of casino chips that I'd never seen before. They were multi-colored, yellow and black like yellow jackets, and the denomination nearly made my knees buckle.

$500,000 per chip.

A lump rose in my throat as I couldn't help but to stand there and count that man's money.

$20 million?

A white guy with a champagne flute walked up beside me and started nodding his head. "That's a pretty good win eh?"

I looked at him like he was crazy. *What did he mean a pretty good hit? That would set anybody for life. What the hell.*

"Yea. That's a great hit. He's on great track to being rich forever."

The white guy glanced up at me and frowned. "Oh nah, he just plays for fun. For the thrill. He'll more than likely gamble it all until he loses it and gives it back."

I really wanted to fight that man for talking foolish to me. That man had won $20 million in what sees like ten minutes and here this other fool come talking about giving it back.

"If he gives back $20 million, that's crazy. I would think 20 million large could help anybody no matter who you were."

The white guy finished his champagne flute and looked at me like I was a small thinking idiot. "$20 million is nothing. The guy is one of the lead angel investors of SnapChat. He's worth billions."

The guy's words echoed in my ear long after he'd walked away from me. I glanced around the room and took a good look at the chips that everyone was gambling with. The minimum chip denomination was valued at $1,000, and they were tossing them across the table as if they were just sprinkling salt on rice. It was a room filled with the who's who of Las Vegas— all big wigs, but no rappers; these were the people who controlled significant chunks of the world.

Social media execs, sports athletes, A-list actors, billionaire socialites— the atmosphere was electric, but I wasn't intimidated in the least bit. Sammy made his way back over to me with a smile on his face. "Devin! There you go my buddy! Are you ready for that withdrawal?"

WINS AND LOSSES

For
the
life
of
me
I
don't
know
how
I
went
from
gambling
with
$1,000
playing
a
game
I'd
never

played
before,
to
being
down
$900,000
over
the
course
of
3 hours.

I was fucking sick! Everything was a blur to me amidst a slightly illuminated version of hell's dungeon. The dealer had scraped the last of my chips into a box, leaving me worst off than I was when I was drinking my pain away. It all seemed unreal. I stood there as if they were going to give it back to me and tell me it was only a joke. At that moment depression slammed into my body like a train going full speed ahead. I had to have a seat because I knew I was going to pass out soon. The room was spinning, and the constant sound of other people cheering because they'd won was driving me insane.

I looked at the dealer like he was my enemy, and he smiled at me as if to tell me I was just another nigga who thought he knew it all. I didn't know how I was going to tell my wife I'd fucked up like this. I hadn't even sent my lawyer the $500,000 he'd requested to keep me and my Pops from going to prison. I closed my eyes and toggled my thoughts, trying to think of a solution to the biggest mess I'd ever made in my life.

I was disappointed in myself as a man. Temptation had lured me in and attacked me, and there I was standing there looking stupid, with temptation's strong grip around my neck. I was fighting for air, but there was none to be had. Everytime I tried to breathe in deep, something cut my breathing short and I found myself taking several series of half-breaths.

A waitress wearing golden body paint walked up to me with a tray in her hands. Her tray was different than the trays that the other waitresses were carrying. Her smile was also different, her voice carried a British accept, and her fragrance was like a light mist of happiness.

"You want one?"

I look in her tray and my eyes bulged when I saw what she was carrying. I just knew that there was no way possible that she was walking around in a public place carrying a tray decorated with packets of cocaine.

"They're free for the high rollers. Take one."

As bad as I was feeling, I needed to grab a few of them. I hadn't used a drug in a year, and I'd made a vow to my wife to make a conscious effort to change, so I couldn't just go out like that... But I was sure that when I told her what I'd done she was going to be beyond pissed.

"No. I'm fine." I lied as I walked over and sat on a stool away from the gambling action. I wished it had all been a dream, but it wasn't. My dumb ass had really lost my entire bank account betting on some stupid ass white ball to land on a dumb ass number. I felt angry. I wondered if they rigged the games so that certain people would always lose. I felt insulted, confused, depressed, suicidal.

The waitress came over and sat beside me. She picked up a baggie of cocaine, opened it up, inserted her stiletto-tip fingernail and dug out some of it.

"Are you sure you're good?" She asked as she put her fingernail to her nose. She vacuumed it— got rid of it off of her fingernail so fast that it was almost as if it never existed there. The coke disappeared just as fast as my money did. I was still staring around the room as if they were going to come out the back and tell me it was all a big joke, but no such thing was happening. People always talk about traumatic experiences in life, having deaths in the family, going to prison, or even going through a divorce... But I'd never experienced a more traumatic experience than losing everything I'd worked hard to have in the blink of an eye.

When I didn't say anything to the waitress, she got up and went to service the rest of the high-rolling cocaine-veined big wigs. It was amazing how many people of power and riches used and abused coke. But what was more amazing was the fact that I'd just fucked my entire life up in only a few moments. I stood up, realizing that nothing was going to change, and pulled my phone out to tell me wife the dumb shit I'd done.

"Hey!" A young Mexican and his friend approached me as I was pulling my wife up on speed dial. I stared at them like they were just as annoying as the rest of the fuckin' people who'd been approaching me.

"Hey."

"My name is Stanton, and this is my friend Altinez. We saw you lost a lot of money playing roulette and would like to help you."

I needed help, but didn't see how they were going to be able to. A part of me was cheering for joy, and another part of me was as skeptical as ever. I didn't have shit to lose though, so I decided to hear them out.

"I'm Devin, but how are you going to help me?" I asked, exhaling and staring at Stanton.

"How much did you lose playing roulette?" Stanton said with a smile on his face.

His demeanor and composure was relaxed and inviting, calming me down and making me lower my guard against the stranger.

"Man I lost nearly a million dollars."

"Yo' I'm sorry to hear that for real." Stanton said, pissing me off. I didn't need his fuckin' pity-party, I need my million back in my account.

"My friend Altinez..." he started, as he sat on the stool next to the one I had been sitting at.

I sat back down and listened to him talk. "My friend Altinez, he lost $3 million playing roulette one week."

I looked at Altinez who was staring blank-faced. Stanton said something in Spanish to Altinez and he nodded his head as to verify what his friend had said to me. I just looked at them both curiously. What the fuck did they want from me? A conversation? I thought as I exhaled.

"I won it back for him though. I won him $10 million in one day. I got back all of his money and helped him profit. See I worked at a casino for 7 years, and I quit once I learned how to beat all their games."

In a time of desperation, he could have told me he had a magic wand that could get all of my money back and I would have gone for it. I'd taken a ridiculous sized loss, and that didn't sit well with me. It was unreal, and I refused to let it exist as reality.

"I'll help you get six times your money back in exchange for 10%." Stanton said as he sat back and folded his arms.

I regarded him for a moment. Curly hair, navy blue business suit with a light grey tie— simple dress shoes, he was fancy enough to fit in, but not doing so much as to stand out and cause any form of suspicion. I stretched my neck right to left. My life was starting to feel better now that I had a legitimate chance at getting my money back. My bad mood was leaving, and happiness had started to show it's smiling face.

"Well aight. What do I need to do, and how long will it take for you to make the money?" I asked, fully interested in the proposition.

"It'll take me like 45 minutes to make it, and you'll need $500,000 worth of chips to get it started."

I didn't want to act like I didn't have it, although I didn't have it at all. I needed to show that I wasn't as bad of a person as I felt. I needed this to work in order to save my life, my family, and possibly, my marriage. I felt like my entire life was on the line at that very moment, and I had no other choice but to come out the victor. I knew God wouldn't let me lose my life like that, so I had the ultimate faith that this was going to work out. However, to get the $500,000...

"Give me a second." I said and stepped away from them. I

called my wife and told her to transfer $500,000 to my account. It had been that simple. She trusted me more than I trusted me. She didn't ask any questions, not what I'm about to do, not even what's my account number– she knew it already, and trusted me with her life. I prayed that I wasn't about to fuck up the only thing I had remaining on this earth– my wife's trust.

Once the money was transferred, I went back to the cage and withdrew it. I had $500,000 worth of chips to gamble with in the span of 30 minutes. The casinos made sure to make the process of gambling your life away as easy and painless as possible. Stanton and Altinez started walking past me towards a small card table in the back with one dealer sitting there.

"Follow me." Stanton said. He didn't have to tell me twice. We all sat down at the table, and I placed my chips on the table.

"What's this game?" I asked curiously.

"It's the best game in the casino. Baccarat. It's the game that James Bond played in his movie." Stanton said matter of factly. "Slide me the chips." I slip them over with no hesitation.

I watched as the dealer started shuffling cards, and I was lost once cards started to hit the table. I watched as Stanton placed an initial bet of $25,000 on the table, my confidence in his luck greater than my confidence in myself. My heart smiled when he won the bet, and I felt myself relax even more. That's $25,000 more than I had to my name, so we definitely were on the right track.

A few bets later Stanton placed a $200,000 bet, and won it as well, taking the total up to $725,000. I sat patiently watching a master at work. He was winning and betting with the confidence of a complete professional, and it seemed like he was unstoppable. He won bet after bet, and never took any big losses throughout the duration.

After about 20 minutes, we were up to $1.5 million– all of my money had been made back and I could get up and get the fuck out of that casino for good. I tapped Stanton on the shoulder.

"That's good homey. Shit we can quit now." I said as I whispered so the dealer wouldn't hear me.

"You wanna quit? I'm on a role... I can get you six times your money back if you want, but if you want me to quit I will. It's up to you."

The logical side had already spoke when I told him we could quit. Anything after that was going to be compulsiveness and spur of the moment tendencies. "Fuck it, let's keep going." I said with a smile on my face.

Before I knew it, we were up to $2 million cash, and I wasn't worried about the size of his bets. He really knew what he was doing in the casino, and I felt like we were going to be the next success story of the day, leaving out with $20 million in cash from a couple of hours' work. The good thing about it all, was I knew I'd made my money back, my wife's money was safe, and I'd profited a half million also. I was so ecstatic, so happy.

Then just like that, he'd lost a $750,000 bet.

I frowned. "What the fuck man?" I mumbled under my breath, but didn't wanna discourage him because he was doing such a great job. I calmed my breathing down and watched as he got set to regroup for the next bet. He nodded his head and smiled.

"I see what happened that time. I was one decision too soon. I'll get it back on this bet." He placed $1.25 million on the table like a professional.

"Wait." I spoke out so the dealer could hear me. "Aye lemme holla at you for a second." I said as I looked at Stanton like he was crazy. Altinez was just as calm as he'd been when they first walked up. Stanton got up and we took a quick walk.

"What's up?" He asked.

"You put all the damn money on the line? Why not put some of it in case you lose?"

"This is bacarrat man. You can't lose this. I was one decision too soon last time, and that's why I lost. I'm telling you I know my stuff man. The last pattern of sequence says this is the next decision."

I had to trust that he knew what he was talking about because I damn sure didn't have a clue. I exhaled, nodded my head, and we walked back to the table. I watched in slow motion as the dealer pulled the cards out of the card shoe, and watched as he dropped a card on the table one by one. I didn't know the game of baccarat, so I didn't know what was going on. The only thing I saw was Stanton squeeze his eyes close in defeat, and I knew it was over.

I nearly blacked out as I watched the dealer in the casino scrape my life off of the table and drop it into a box. I was done. Cooked. I couldn't even be angry at nobody but myself. I turned and started walking and Stanton stopped me.

"Hey Devin. It's the next card man. Don't give up now. Do you have another $500,000? We can get it all back right now."

I finally saw that man for what he was. He was no different than me. An addict. A broke man addicted to something that he couldn't afford— the constant chase of a thrill, the pursuit of a roller coaster ride that we didn't meet the minimum emotional requirements to embark on. We were one and the same. Both pitiful, both helpless, both naïve, both lost, both sucked in by bright lights and illusions of grandeur. As angry as I was for him, I felt just as sorry for him as I'd felt for myself.

I didn't know his life path, or what difficulties and bad decisions led him to a chance meeting with me in Las Vegas, but I knew that this was by far the deepest test that I'd ever been administered. I shook my head in pity, both for him and for me. I shook my head as I walked away with full intentions to never see him again. As I walked out of the door, the casino host crossed paths with me with a smile on his face.

"Have a great day, better luck to you!" He said with a small chuckle. It was almost as if they had all conspired against me the moment I'd entered Caesar's Palace. From the constant offers of free and endless cocaine, the offers of free alcohol, the conversations about money and success, the coaxing, the illusions of VIP treatment— all the way down to Stanton and Altinez. I'd failed my biggest test to date with a big fat goose egg.

I walked to the elevator feeling like I was drunk, even though I was completely sober. My lawyer sent me a text asking me if I got the situation handled, but it was nothing I could say. I blocked his number. I couldn't afford him, so I would have to just accept whatever happened to me as a result. I saw that I had an email from the studio, 9 completed songs from Black Barbee, but my energy was so low that I didn't even listen to the tracks. Instead I forwarded the songs to my publicist and turned my phone off.

I got off the elevator and walked to my hotel room defeated. I felt like I'd just gone through a heavyweight fight with life and lost in the first round. Fittingly, I was sure many people had lost to the elusive city of Las Vegas in the first round, but it didn't make me feel any better. I walked in the room and straight to the bed. My wife was at the desk typing when I laid down. I closed my eyes without speaking a word.

"What's wrong?" She asked.

I couldn't say shit. I was so angry at myself that I couldn't even find the words. She saw the look on my face and automatically knew the entire story.

"Please tell me you didn't have me send you a half million dollars so that you could gamble." She said calmly.

For the life of me, I had never been able to figure out how women always knew. Maybe it was a sense that they were blessed with, similar to touch, sight, hearing, smelling, tasting– the 6th sense of a woman was *knowing*.

I closed my eyes as I listened to my wife start crying hysterically. I didn't need her to tell me that I'd let her down, I knew this before I even made it to the hotel room. She walked slowly to the corner of the room adjacent to where I was laying, put her face in her palms, and cried.

"Devin how could you?" Her cracked voice penetrated my soul like a poisonous dagger. The truth was, I couldn't even explain myself. I was hiding one cover up with a fuck-up, one mistake after the other. I wasn't good enough to be her husband, nor did I deserve the title. I closed my eyes and listened to her cry in pain of being let down.

She had real tears, not tears from a small mistake being exaggerated into something big, but from the reality that I'd really shattered the most sacred thing we had for each other- trust. I kept my eyes closed to trap my own tears in, I squeezed them tight as she cried harder. Her weeps of pain sharper than my pain from shame. I squeezed my lips together in defeat. It wasn't the first time I'd ever been defeated in life, but it was for sure my most painful. It was my most painful because it was no longer me being affected by my stupidity, but a woman I'd vowed before God to owner. I was a dishonor, a loser, a lame, ashamed in more ways than two.

I squeezed my eyes tighter, so that the tears would flow down the inside of my soul and wash the sadness away.

The tears flowed inside of me. Quietly I hurt, while she hurt in surround sound.

"Devin I trusted you!" She screamed in tears before getting up and walking into the bathroom, shutting the door, and shutting out the possibility for any reply from me.

Trusted.

That sentence probably hurt me worse than any loss I'd taken in my life.

That one word tore my soul to shreds, ripped my once hard ego and self-esteem into lettuce pieces, although it still wasn't easy to digest nor was it good for me in any way. I exhaled, and fell asleep in that same position.

Shame-sleep. It was the nap you took when you had no more answers to life. It was the closest thing you could do to leave the earth outside of physically harming yourself. Relief only came during my sleep of shame.

TERRANCE

Me and Barbee had walked around the Las Vegas strip all evening before we found some more shit. I'd pre-judged crack cocaine and everyone who used it in the past, mainly because of the stigma surrounding it. When I saw a picture of a crack-head, it was normally a busted down homeless person with dirty clothes and missing teeth. That wasn't the case with us. We had money so we could always afford it and we kept ourselves together. Maybe the people who made crack a priority over all other responsibilities shouldn't be using it. Crack wasn't our top priority; it was only a recreational thing that we happened to both like.

We headed back to the room hand in hand once we had enough for the both of us. I hadn't heard from my son since I sent him the songs, but I didn't wanna' bother him on his vacation. He needed to enjoy that with his wife. My phone rang and I sent it to voicemail without looking to see who it was. It rang again, and I glanced at it to see, but when I didn't recognize the number or have it saved, I sent it back to voicemail.

TERRANCE

We walked for about 5 more minutes when a text message came through to my phone. I exhaled and opened the text.

How dare you Mr. Terrance. You and your son are just alike, and I'm so disappointed in the both of you. There is nothing you or him can say to me right now, and I am so ashamed! I'm soooo ashamed! I pray that that young man's life was worth taking when you're sitting in that prison reflecting on your sins. All I can do is pray for you and for your son. I pray that God touches the both of you in a way that only God Almighty can. I'm so hurt by this I can't even believe it.

I was initially nonchalant while reading Ashlon's text because I knew that she really didn't know anything, until I got to the end of the text message. My hands started shaking as I stared at The Shade Room's screenshot of me coming out of Drum Killer's place the night of his murder. I was crushed. Mainly crushed because I knew I'd let my son down, and even more crushed because I knew I was about to be snatched from Black Barbee and buried in a prison cell somewhere.

"You ok OG?" Barbee said with a smile on her face.

I didn't know what to say to her honestly. Hell nah I wasn't ok, but she didn't need to know that right away. I had a few questions for her, and depending on how she answered those questions were going to determine my next actions.

"Barbee do you love me?"

She looked at me surprisingly. "I mean... We kinda just met, but I could see myself falling in love one day... Maybe..."

Maybe was better than no. I thought about the possible ways to get out of my jam, and knew that the only way out would be to give up my son and let the authorities know that it was his orders that I was following. Maybe if I did that, they would give us both less time. He wouldn't get as much time as me because his record wasn't bad, but if I took the charge straight up, they were going to bury me and I was never going to see Barbee again.

"What's wrong Terrance?"

I shook my head. "Nothing we need to worry about right now." I walked faster to get off the streets and out of everyone's face. I needed to get high to clear my thoughts of the negative stuff so I could come up with the best solution to my problems. I heard Barbee's phone go off, but I thought nothing of it. We needed to hurry to the room, the hell with a phone.

"Wait slow down." Barbee said as she stared wide-eyed at a small candy store adjacent to the hotel. "I gotta get some cotton candy. Wait right here, don't go anywhere." She jetted into the store and I stood outside waiting nervously. Another text came to my phone and I opened it angrily to see what it was about.

God always forgives. I told my Pastor all about you and he still wants to meet you. It doesn't matter when you give your life to God, and accept Jesus Christ; just as long as you do it before you leave this earth. I pray for you Terrance. I really do. I know you don't like me pressuring you, but God told me you were fighting a fight that only he would be able to help you with, and I wanted to deliver all the information I could before it was too late. I'm sorry if I came across the wrong way, but I really had high hopes that we could one day–

I deleted her text message without reading it all. I was tired of her texting me. After it was successfully deleted, I blocked her number so that she couldn't contact me again at all. I had a growing relationship with Barbee, and I intended on staying with her for the rest of my days. I was in love, and I was sure that we were going to have a beautiful family together one day. As soon as I placed my phone in my pocket it rang. I was pissed, and about to take that damn phone and break it in half, but out of curiosity and boredom of waiting on Barbee to come out the store, I answered it.

"Hello?"

"Yes sirrrr." Banny's dark, ominous voice vibrated in my ears. He was calling me from either a private number or he'd changed his phone number just to call me. What a fool.

"Yes sir what?" I asked him. "You're still jealous of me Banny? You mad because I used your information to get out and now I'm living my best life? You're sillier than I thought. Why are you calling me anyways?"

"If I told you I prayed about this situation, what would you say?" Banny said, his voice reeking of arrogance and assurance.

"I can always use a prayer, so thanks." I said nonchalantly.

Banny laughed a low, ominous chuckle. "Alright, and if I told you I called the root man about you, what would you say then?"

I exhaled. I knew his Jamaican roots, and knew he was serious as a heart attack about the root man. "Why would you put roots on me man?" I asked, suddenly wondering if that was why the sudden wave of bad luck was washing over me.

"You see?" Banny said in a serious tone. "See you ain't never grow up Terrance. For a man of your age to be more afraid of me calling the root man than me going to God about this situation— your priorities are completely messed up. You're more afraid of the devil and black magic than you are of God's wrath. That's a serious problem, and it's going to take a sacrifice on your behalf to make it all right— that's if it's not too late for you. You see I'm done with you. I don't have anything else to do or say to you, but I am going to say that you're dead wrong for betraying our friendship."

I could hear the hurt in his voice, and I started to realize that he wasn't really hurt that I'd used the information to get myself out, but that I didn't keep my end of the bargain and stay in contact with him like I told him I would. I tried to picture myself in his shoes, and I realized that I would be just as pissed at him as he was at me. Despite all of it, I couldn't bring myself to tell him I was sorry. Fuck him. He was just as cold hearted a criminal as anybody else, what the hell right did he have to be talking about God like he knew Him better than anybody else.

"You through talking?" I was annoyed. Fuck all that talking.

He hung up without further comment. I looked up and saw Barbee standing in the window with her cotton candy in her hand. I looked at her beautiful features, soft skin, soft eyes, gorgeous even-toned complexion, perfect breasts– She was the most amazing woman I'd ever laid eyes on. I smiled at her.

She didn't smile back, and instead just stared at me. I held my hands out asking her what the issue was and trying to figure out why she was just standing there. When she didn't reply, I started walking towards the glass door entrance to the candy shop. I pulled the door and it wouldn't budge. I pulled again thinking that I wasn't pulling hard enough, then realized that it was locked.

I pointed at the door. "Barbee open the door."

She stared at me and shook her head as if she didn't give a fuck.

I was confused.

I stared at her through the glass window, my heart pounding against my chest as my soul reached out for the woman I loved. I knew she felt the same about me, there was no other way. How could she not? We were perfect together.

"Freeze! Hands up! Hands up!"

I didn't even budge when I heard the police. I continued to stare at Barbee even though she'd ripped my heart out of my body. I can't believe she called the police on me without even so much as a conversation to get my perspective on things. And to think... I was about to give my son up for her because we loved each other. I was a fool.

"Hands up! Final warning!"

I put my hands up and dropped to my knees.

"Hands behind your back! Behind your back!"

I placed my hands behind my back and the officers moved in and arrested me. I forgot I had the crack cocaine in my pocket also, so that was about to be a whole other charge on top of my murder charge. The moment they clasped the handcuffs around my wrist was the moment they unclasped the lock on the door to the candy shop. I stared at Barbee one final time, nodding my head in acknowledgement to the fact that I'd just got taken, used, and finessed. She had the deal she wanted, and she played on my weakness– her.

She'd drowned my sense of reality with her charming ways, good looks, and hard drugs. It wasn't her fault however...

Me and my son were one and the same. Our anger mirrored each others and that was a lethal combination. He would get so angry that he couldn't control himself, and he got it honest. I could have changed my ways when I was younger and I didn't. My example was put out into the world only to come back and bite me with its venomous fangs. I had one chance and ruined it.

Barbee walked past me as if she didn't even know me. I stared in disbelief, and felt sick knowing that I was on the verge of giving up my son for someone who would give me up for nothing. I watched as she shook hands with a detective and took his card. I got into the back seat of the cop car, the procedure a familiar to me. As the car drove off, I thought about all of the chances I had to get it right, all of the opportunities I had to give me life to God, all of the warnings, close calls, and prayer offers that had come my way. It seemed as though I turned down all prayers and embraced the claws of the devil.

As ironic as that was, I still sent a prayer up for my son.
    I prayed that he changed, no matter what it took to change him. I was going to clear his name in the murder, and just take the charge myself. It's the least I could do since it was my mistake. I could have just told him that wasn't the right way to go and cleared both of our conscious, but I didn't. I had one last chance to guide him and raise him up, and I still failed, so I accepted the fact that it was time for me to pay for my failures.

DEVIN

I woke up that night with a vicious headache. When I saw the time I couldn't believe that I'd slept the entire evening away, but when the memory of my bad decision making came flooding back, I really wanted to just go back to sleep. I lay in the dark silence thinking about how I'd failed the only successful thing I'd ever truly had- my wife. It hurt me to hurt her, and I knew she deserved an apology. I reached over to put my arms around her, but to my surprise my arm hit the empty mattress.

Although the hotel room was dark, I saw a glimmer of light coming from the bathroom, so I figured she was there. I got up, made my way to the bathroom and opened the door- but she wasn't there. I went back to the dresser and grabbed my cell phone so I could call her. I dialed her number, and to my surprise, her phone rang from inside of the room. I walked into the living room to where I heard the phone ringing, but to my surprise, she wasn't there and had left the phone behind.

Under the phone was a letter to me, and the moment I saw her handwriting is when panic began to truly set in. I'd experienced a lot of pain in my life, had done a lot of bad things- but I really didn't intend to be such a bad person. I'm more reactionary than action... Meaning I went with the flow until prompted to respond to something. Mentally, I felt like a deer walking across 100 lanes worth of highway, stopping every single time I saw a bright light or a shiny object. If that was me mentally, then that letter in front of me was my first major highway wreck. It was wrinkled from water damage, almost like a sheet of paper that had been rained upon.

Devin,

God only knows the depths of how I love you. My husband, my best friend, my comforter; my everything. God only knows how I feel about you, because the very moment I try to put it in words, no matter which words I use and regardless of how great I try to decorate my explanation, it's still not strong enough to show you my love. I love you to death. I love you beyond death, and beyond whatever is after the after-life. So it really hurts me to have to write this letter to you.

First I need you to understand that this isn't about the money you lost gambling and this isn't about me having second thoughts about being your wife. What this is about however, is trust. See Devin I prayed for a man like you, and God answered my prayer. God is also the same God I pray to each and every day, it never fails and I'll never stop praying to Him. He is my savior, my Father— the only person who could ever mean more to me than my family. You see Devin... I knew what the possibility was before we even got to Las Vegas, so the only hurt part about it for me was that you actually fell victim to the temptation.

This isn't what hurt me the most though. What broke me down spiritually is your anger. Your self control. See... you'll let someone or something anger you to the point where you're willing to sacrifice your entire family to get revenge. That's not right Devin. I don't want to feel like I'm not worth it. I don't want to feel like I can be loved one moment and sacrificed the next moment because of your pride. I don't want to feel like I can lose you any moment simply because of your unwillingness to put things in the Lord's hand and not yours or your father's.

Devin... God wants me to walk away from you right now.

I don't know how long, or what's the true reasoning, because that's between you and Him. All I know is this is the heaviest thing on my spirit and I refuse to ignore my spirit even though I hate this. I hate having to walk away from you for even 10 minutes, so you know if I'm walking away from you, this is an order that came straight from the Almighty and directly into my heart. I'm crying as I write this because I don't want to leave you, but I know the penalty for disobeying God's orders.

I'm going back home to try to fix whatever I can possibly fix. I need you to get on your knees and have a conversation with God unlike any exchange you've ever had in your life. I need you to get on your knees in silence and darkness and pray to Him until the only sounds you hear are from God's mouth to your ears, and the only light is the brightness of His presence. I need you to take your time and listen to God, let Him use you, heal you, ask Him to bring you out of this while you still have a chance.

I'll be home waiting on you Devin, but don't cheat the process. Only you will know when God has spoken to you, and only you'll know when to come home as the man God wanted you to be. Don't worry about the girls, they're going to love you if it's the last thing I ever teach them. The fact that I'm willing to obey God despite my own desires— this is a sample of what I want from you Devin. I want you to obey God despite your own desires. Baby I love you, and that will never change. I'm sorry the paper is so wrinkled up, but I've been crying since I picked up the ink pen.

I'll be in Georgia at our house, waiting on God to make it a home again. My life will not be ok until you're back by my side. I wanna say hurry Devin... But I know God's lessons aren't lessons of speed, but lessons of accuracy. See you soon.

Your Wife— Ashlon.

I was crushed. Tears ran from my face as if they were scared of me. For the first time in my life, I was scared, alone, hurt and abandoned.

"Why you keep picking on me God?" I cried into the empty room. I tried to read the letter again, but I couldn't even see it because my tears kept blocking my vision. I lay back on the sofa in the darkness and cried a cry longer and harder, deeper and strong than I'd ever cried in my life. This wasn't about money or fame, wasn't about success or love— this was about pain. That letter was the single most difficult letter I'd ever read in my life. To say that it broke my heart was an understatement.

No matter how crushed I was, I knew that letter was the truth. I knew my wife loved me enough to not let me lose my soul, and cared for me enough to help me save myself. Most women didn't understand the difference between loving a man and caring for a man, and most didn't even know that there was a difference. You can tell a man you love him as many times as you please or desire, and you may mean it or may not mean it... But that didn't mean you *cared* for him.

Caring for him to want him to be the best version of himself. Caring for his emotional needs the way a woman wanted her own emotional needs cared for. Women wanted to be cared for, but not care for. Once upon a time, a black woman was the most at-risk person in the United States of America. It was a black man's duty to protect his woman and care for her in a world that did not. As times changed, a black man became the most at-risk person instead of the black woman. A black man's value is often tainted by social media opinions, memes, songs promoting why a woman doesn't need a black man— Rejection from society, rejection from corporate America, rejection from his black women— the alienation of a black man is the most common type of hidden abuse in the country.

You would never know because a black man isn't going to show his emotional side for fear of seeming weak in a world controlled by dominance.

Women are abused by abused men.

Women are not abused by men who are not or have not been abused. A newborn black male comes out craving a black woman, not abusing a black woman. Abuse is taught to others by the abused. Love is natural.

There was a new Bible sitting on the table with a golden bow on it. I pulled the strand the release the bow, and opened it up randomly. It was dark, so I took my phone and shined the flashlight to the passage I'd opened up to. When I read it, I knew my wife was the truth, and that God spoke to me through her. I read the passage and knew that He wanted me to be closer to Him instead of the world. My phone had been vibrating since I woke up, and I had so many unread text messages in my phone that I didn't even wanna read them. Based on what my wife said in the letter, I knew what was going on with my Dad already, and it was nothing I could do about the situation but wait on God's decisions. I read the random passage aloud in the darkness.

Isaiah 55:6 13
Seek the LORD while he may be found; call upon him while he is near; let the wicked forsake his way, and the unrighteous man his thoughts; let him return to the LORD, that he may have compassion on him, and to our God, for he will abundantly pardon. For my thoughts are not your thoughts, neither are your ways my ways, declares the LORD.

I read the passage several times slowly, giving each word extra thought to make sure that I understood it correctly. If it wasn't too late, I was about to get my life together on an entirely different level. I needed to open my heart and allow God in on a scale unlike any He'd ever used me before. I prayed the rest of the night, and asked God for direction and sound decision making. I asked him for patience and understanding, and for a safety net against the temptations of the world.

THE JOURNEY

The first thing I did when I woke up the next day was go look for a church. I didn't need to ask anybody where to go, or get any recommendations because I was riding with my spiritual GPS system. I had a credit card with a $15,000 credit limit on it, so I was going to survive off of that as best as I could and as long as I needed to. The rental car I was in was of a completely different league than the Bentley trucks and Rolls Royces I was used, but for the first time in my adult life I no longer cared about my material image.

I drove all morning Sunday, writing down churches and addresses, trying to determine which church gave me the best energy, what church pulled me towards it so that I could park and get out. In a city that advertised itself as a city of sin, I was still expecting to find a church that was meant for me, and which church had the message that God wanted me to receive. I'd drove around Vegas so long that the churches were letting out and I was still writing down church names. I hated the fact that I didn't actually go to church that day, but when it came to taking a journey in life, every detail in the travel route affected the destination.

Some type of way I ended up getting lost in my route, and I found myself driving through a residential neighborhood instead of being on the main street per my intentions. Once I made it to the end of the street, there was an older black man and older black woman outside of a tattered and beat up looking building talking to a small group of people. It was only about 14 people outside total, but I was intrigued immediately.

With it only being 14 people, I knew that the church wasn't in business trying to get rich and disguising their intentions by telling everyone they wanted to spread God's word to as many people as possible. It didn't take millions of dollars to accomplish what God had already written. I parked my rental car in the driveway, got out and started walking towards the small crowd. As I got closer I could see that the youngest person had to be around 55 years old. I was the youngest person on the property.

"Mayyyy I help you?" The older gentleman spoke out. His face was wrinkled of experience, his hair gray of knowledge, and his voice was seasoned with honesty and respect. All of the things he had is what I wanted to learn how to have in life.

"Yes. My name is Devin..." I said, suddenly getting nervous. It was weird that I'd performed in front of hundreds of thousands of fans at once with no problem, but I was shaking like a cat that just jumped out of a swimming pool in front of the 14 people in front of me.

"God sent me here." I didn't know what else to say. I prayed that I didn't offend them, as my intentions weren't bad, I just really wanted to be a better person.

"Yes. We know." The older guy said gently. The congregation parted as him and the woman he was standing besides started taking steps towards me.

"You're broken." The woman said once they got in front of me. "You're torn and confused."

I stared speechless. I was about to say something, but didn't.

"You've been gambling." The guy said as if he was reading from my diary. I wasn't that impressed however, because I *was* in Las Vegas, so I'm pretty sure he met people who had gambling problems every day.

"Your wife left you? I see sadness. Sadness not from losing money gambling, but sadness from a broken heart." The older lady was on point.

"We are not a church young one." The old man said as he stared into my eyes. "We are just a group of spiritual advisers, and my wife here is a prophet. We only come here to meet after church. Just us amongst each other. What I will tell you however, is that you haven't gotten right with the Lord yet."

I could feel the tears starting to form because I knew he was right. I still believed in vengeance and revenge, my heart was still tainted with the residue of street rules.

"I wanna get right with the Lord." I said. "I really do. I'm making an effort."

"Stop making an effort and make a decision." The woman's voice was sharp and no-nonsense. "You wanna hurt people who do you wrong. I can see it on your face. How can you get right with the Lord when you wanna play God?"

The older man stepped back when she said that, his eyes wide-eyed, his face startled. He looked concerned as his wife continued to speak.

"Your past! You've been playing God hurting people to where they can't pray anymore."

The small crowd gasped. Tears filled my eyes as I thought about the orders of revenge I'd placed in the streets over the years.

"You've been taking people away from their families!" Tears started flowing from the lady's eyes and it scared me to death but I knew that everything happened for a reason, and I wasn't hearing any of this by accident.

"You have the devil in you but you say God sent you! You've been doing the devil's work while telling God that you want Him to use you to do His. Look at you. You make mother's and father's cry while you cry when things don't work out for you! You want help, but what about the people who can't ask for help anymore because you took that away from them?"

She was passionate and accurate, my tears burned my eyes as I stood there and listened to my truths.

"Your wife deserves better than you."

Her words were cutting me deep, but I knew she was right. "She deserves better, but she knows that God is a forgiving God. She deserves better but she feels that God is going to restore you. You won't get restored until you go to him completely. You owe it to every person you've ever hurt who can no longer ask for forgiveness for their own sins... You owe it to them to ask for forgiveness of your own sins."

I couldn't even get a word out for the tears flowing down my face.

THE JOURNEY

I'd been a coward during times when I was supposed to be a man. Instead of me handling my problems correctly or coming to God with my issues, I'd ran to the streets, paying people to hurt people— sometimes beyond repair. When I paid people to hurt people, I could finally see that my actions always hurt more people than the intended targets or victims.

"Your past." The lady's arms started shaking and her voice started trembling. "Your past has your future in prison! You can't and won't stop having bad luck in life until you break the bondages of your past sins. Get forgiveness and grow. Change your life so that you can truly help people, and not just help people when it was convenient for you or when everything was going good for you. Change your life so you can help people with more than money."

I stood before the small group of people uncertain of what to say in response. I didn't know if I was supposed to apologize or say thank you— and before I could utter a word, the lady held her hand up to silence me.

"There is nothing you need to say to us young man. The only person you need to talk to is God. I can sense that he's broken you once before, and he pulled you out. He broke you to show you his wrath and his power. He clearly has a big purpose for you, otherwise He wouldn't keep bending and pulling you. You better go to Him voluntarily while He's asking for you!"

I put my head down in silence. Everything she'd said to me was right. I had to stop feeling bad about my bad luck streaks and change my life once and for all. I nodded my head in acceptance of my past failures. What was supposed to only be a vacation in the city of sin had become the trip that could potentially save my life.

"Young man..." The older man's voice lowered as he stared at me intensely. "He's not going to give you too many warnings... If you don't change when you know better— you haven't seen even a glimpse of God's wrath and fury. You see... it's a difference of when you're doing wrong and don't know better... But make no mistake about it... When you know for a fact that you're going against what God has told you... I wouldn't wanna be around when the ground opens up on you."

GEORGIA

I was born and raised in Georgia, not from Atlanta where me and my wife and kids currently lived, but from a one red-light town that nobody had ever heard of before. If I told you the name of the town, you wouldn't remember it the next day. The population was only 2,000, it was the type of community that had more churches than restaurants, and more graveyards than parks. Cultural, a place that held you accountable for your actions because everyone knew you and your family.

After leaving Las Vegas, I made the decision to return to my hometown– a place I hadn't shown my face in much since becoming a famous entertainer, but it was the one place that would always feel the safest for me. It was the only place in the world that held my secrets and never sold them to the public. It was a place where if you did something outrageous or crazy, or if you acted a way you knew you weren't supposed to act, ain't no tellin' who's Grandma, Aunt, Mom, or Uncle would come have a sit-down with you to get yourself together.

The phrase *it takes a village to raise a child*, was most poignant in my hometown.

I had an Aunt and Uncle who were 82 and 83 years old. Aunt

Annie-Mae and Uncle Johnny. The last time I'd seen them was when I came through the town early in my successful career to show off my new Ferrari. I remember them not being impressed by the car, but more impressed with me being a healthy man living his life. I think that was what drove me away and kept me away– not the Ferrari... But the way they didn't care about the success that Atlanta cared about. I wanted to be in a place that cared about the success, so I could hear my praises every day. That was crazy when I thought about it because this was a place that gave me praises when I had no success at all. I needed that– not the praises, but I needed to be around realness.

I stood on the steps and knocked on my Aunty's trailer door. In my hometown, people didn't lock their doors, nor did they even close them until it was time to go to sleep. The main door was open and it was only a screen door separating the cold world from their warm home.

"Who is it?" I heard my Uncle's voice carry through the house.

"Devin!" I said so he could hear me.

"Devin? Who is Devin?"

I'd already forgotten that nobody in my hometown called me Devin or Q Mack or Q Money or any of that. They all called me by my nickname.

"It's Bear-Bear!" I said, and laughed. If the world knew that there were people who called me Bear-Bear, they would never let me live it down. But in my hometown I could live it up.

"Bear-Bear that's you?" He wasn't moving too well at his old-age, and I felt ashamed for not coming to visit him and my Aunty sooner. I listened as he made a slow-motion effort to make it from the kitchen table to the front door to where I was standing. The only thing separating me from coming in was a tiny latch that I could easily just pop open, but instead I stood patiently and waited for him to unhook it.

"Ohhhh my Looyyyyd! I can't believe it! Bear-Bear!" He said as a smile took over his face. "Annie Mae! You not finna' believe this!"

"What is it Johnny?" I heard my Aunty holler from the bathroom.

"Bear Bear is here at our place!" He screamed back.

"Whatttt?" I heard the toilet flush and the sink come on, and I heard her talking but couldn't make out what she was saying over the sound of the water combined with the distance.

Uncle Johnny finally opened the door and let me in. I walked in and put my hands out to shake his, he grabbed my hand and pulled me in for a hug. My defenses disappeared as his fragile arms held me as tight as they could. This was the love I'd been missing in my life. The love of people who wanted nothing from you.

"Boy we missed you down here! Me and your Aunt, we missed you boy!" I didn't expect him to start crying, and I didn't expect to start crying either.

My Aunt made her way to where we were and as soon as my Uncle got through hugging me, my Aunt put her fragile arms around me also. "Welcome home Bear-Bear!" She was crying too. It was almost as if they knew I needed them, almost as if they knew I needed those hugs, that type of love, and to be shown that I really matter in life.

"We're so happy you came by to see us!" My Uncle wiped his eyes while walking to the sofa to get off of his feet. I could tell that the simple walk to the screen door from the kitchen had taken a toll out of him, I could tell that he was tired, exhausted.

"I'm just as happy that I'm here." I said as I wiped my eyes and put a smile on my face. I really loved them, despite the fact that it had been nearly ten years since I'd been there the last time. An entire decade of life had passed us by, ten years of separation yet our bond was closer than the people I saw every single day of my life. The connection was stronger to them than all of my fans combined, despite them not ever caring for my music at their age.

"I know you probably real busy and about to leave, but if you stick around for an hour I'll cook you some pork chop." My Aunty said as she walked to the kitchen and opened the freezer.

"I don't eat pork." I said.

"Boy hush. You eat pork. You ate it your whole life and loved it. Don't let the world change you when you can change the world. I know you're in a hurry, but if you can just give me an hour I'll have this cooked up real good for you."

I looked around their small worn down single-wide trailer, and wondered why I never offered to have them a house built when I could have easily made that happen. I made a mental note to surprise them with a new place as soon as I could get back on my feet good.

"Well actually... I was trying to see if y'all would let me stay with y'all for a few weeks. Maybe two weeks... Not even a whole two weeks."

They stared at me in silence and confusion. I could see that they were stunned that I'd made such a request. It was a humble request, one that I didn't see coming out of my mouth in a million years.

"Bear-Bear you're welcome to stay here as long as you want. You can stay here forever if you want." Aunty said as she smiled at me. "I'm sorry my house is a mess, but I can clean up the guest room so you can have some privacy. Johnny's old fishing poles are in there but we—"

Uncle Johnny started to get up off of the sofa. "I'ma go move them fishing poles and stuff out the way for you."

"No... I'll do it Uncle Johnny, you have a seat." I walked back and helped him sit down on the sofa. "I'll handle it. I'll clean it up y'all don't worry."

My Aunt was staring at me like she saw a ghost. "Baby you ok? Why are your eyes so red?"

"Oh. Yea I'm ok. I just gotta get some rest, that's all."

"Alright then. Well don't ignore your body Bear Bear. That's what your Uncle did all those years I told him not to. That's why we gotta go to the doctor every week for them to work on his arthritis and high-blood pressure."

"I'll be aight. Them doctors don't know what they talking about." He said with a grunt.

"If they didn't know what they were doing we wouldn't be going." My Aunty rebutted.

"What I'ma do with your Aunty young jap? I been putting up with her stuff for going on 63 years now."

"It would have been 64 years if you hadn't have cheated on me when I left you back in–"

"Ohhh hear we go. Let it go woman!"

I started laughing. I'd never seen a love as strong and pure as theirs, and it made me proud to witness what my bloodline looked like at its greatest. One day that was going to be me and Ashlon.

"Where is your wife? Ain't you married? You ain't even brought her down here so she could meet us? We would have came to the wedding but you know we weren't tryna get on no planes for that fancy marriage y'all had. A boy at the store showed me y'all wedding pictures on the computer one day. Y'all looked good chile! We so proud of you!"

I didn't know how to answer that question, but I didn't want to not say anything. "My wife is doing well. Aunty when the next time y'all going to church?"

My Aunt dropped a cup in the sink by accident when I asked about church. I hadn't been to Lemrock Baptist Church in at least 15 good years. I stopped going when I was 14 years old and made excuses every Sunday when my family wanted me to go.

"We got revival this week starting tonight. We'll be going every day this week. You going with us?"

"Yes I am."

If I'd done nothing else in life, I knew that I'd made my Aunty and Uncle happy.

"Well we got a few hours before we leave for church, so make yourself at home son." My Uncle had this big grin on his face, and I had the same one in response.

"Y'all got a lawn mower?"

"It's a lawn mower in that there shed. It's a boy who be coming to cut our grass once a month–"

"Supposedly once a month." Aunty interrupted.

"Well yea supposedly. He hadn't been here the last two months so that grass just been growing and growing."

※

I hadn't cut grass since I was 13 years old. The rest of the world knew me as a major celebrity, or knew me as a really bad person depending on who you asked, but my Aunt and Uncle remembered back when I got paid my first $10 to cut their grass. As I cut their lawn with their push mower I thought back to those days. Back then $10 was a lot of money. I'd cut their lawn and felt like I was rich because I was able buy what seemed like an unlimited amount of honey buns and sodas.

I cut their grass thinking about my childhood, all of my deepest memories tickling my mind as they resurfaced. After I was done mowing their yard I was going to clean the trash up out of their yard. I saw where my Aunty had tried to start planting a small garden but the upkeep of it wasn't that good. There were a lot of weeds that were there and I was going to clean that up for her too. They weren't able to move around like they once did, but they still liked the same activities. I was going to help them as much as I could while being there.

I finished the yard and looked at the grass stains on my white Versace sneakers. I laughed because if they knew how much I'd paid for those shoes they would whoop me for cutting grass in them. I didn't care anymore though; image was no longer my concern. My only concern was walking in God's image.

I put the lawn mower back in the small wooden shed and grabbed my things out of the small compact rental car. I walked back into their trailer and smiled at my Aunty, who was finished with the pork chops.

"Dinner's ready. Baby I gotta lay down and get me some rest before church. I'ma be on my feets and things at church so I gots to be real rested. Your Uncle went to sleep as soon as you went out that door. He was real tired."

"Thank you Aunty. I appreciate you for letting—"

"Don't thank me child. Thank you for cutting our grass." Her voice got lower. "Bear Bear... don't say nothing because he didn't want nobody to know... but your Uncle Johnny is real sick these days ok?"

Her voice was cracked as she said it, and it made me feel bad to hear it. I didn't wanna have that conversation at that moment, so I saved my questions about what was wrong. I only wanted to focus on the love and the happiness, I didn't want to dwell on the pain and suffering of life, and I didn't want them to dwell on it either.

"It's going to be ok Aunty. I got a lot of faith these days."

"That's what I'm talking about boy!" She had a huge smile on her face. "I'm right there with ya! The biggest faith I ever had in all of my days." After she said it, she immediately seemed like she was out of energy.

"Go ahead and get your rest Aunty. I'm about to go get ready for church."

※

I loved my wife so much that I cried when I thought of her.

It had been nearly 5 days since I'd head from or saw her, but my wedding ring kept me company when I wasn't in her presence. That ring carried memories with it— a circular treasure box with some of the greatest moments ever seeping its energy through the eons of the metal.

It hurt me that I'd hurt her, but now that I was experiencing what real hurt felt like, I never wanted to hurt another person ever again in my life. I wanted nothing but love to be the bridge from one day to the next. I thought about my daughters, and missed them greatly, but I knew that the path I had been on would have made me miss them every day for eternity. I was glad to have the opportunity to change.

I sat down on the small bed and turned my phone on after having it off for three days straight. The first thing I did was check the news to see what was going on with my Pops. The old me blamed him for making the mistake he made when he carried out my orders, but the new me knew that the mistake was mine and mine only. It was something I was going to pray about and ask for forgiveness for. I needed a new understanding delivered unto me. That rapper had disrespected me in front of my kids, and as a result, I'd ordered his death. I needed God to show me how to deal with my anger. I was willing to take whatever test I needed to take to clean my thoughts.

I hated that I'd sent my father back to prison, and hated that I'd sent Drum Killer away from this earth before he could have a chance to mature. I'd had him killed when I was no better than he was from a maturity standpoint. We were immature in different ways. Him who wanted to impress his friends, and me who wanted to walk with God with one foot and kick street vengeance with the other.

The article I was reading said that my father was going to accept a guilty plea for a lesser charge of manslaughter. They were going to give him less time since he was saving the tax payers money for the trial, plus it made the prosecutor's office look good because they would get the conviction they needed under their belts. The tone was really carefree since it was just another black man who got killed by another black man. They didn't treat it with the type of outrage or concern if it had been a white man involved. There would have been no manslaughter charges in a case with a white man— the charge would have been murder and they would have been seeking the maximum penalty.

I kept scrolling to catch up with what I'd missed. I saw that my PR had released some songs from Black Barbee's mixtapes, and they'd took the world by storm. She had the number 1 song on iTunes already and God knows I needed that money. I was holding on to my last lil' bit amount of money. I called my entertainment lawyer so that I could get a financial estimate of how much money I was going to make off of Black Barbee's song.

"Hey Devin! I've been trying to get in contact with you! Are you ok?"

"Yea I'm fine Donny. Listen... What type of profit am I looking at with Black Barbee's record sales?"

"Yeaaaaa you must have been laying really really low if you haven't heard what's happened. See that's why I've been trying to contact you Devin, you need someone checking on you who cares about your well-being *plus* your financial interests."

"Huh?" I really just wanted to know how much money I was about to profit, I didn't really wanna talk about any rumors.

"Well I'm not sure how much you know or don't know... They found Black Barbee dead a few days ago. You didn't know this? She overdosed on crack cocaine in Las Vegas."

I put my hand over my mouth in shock. It further magnified how bad of a person I was for not even taking the time to talk to her. Maybe I could have saved her life with a simple conversation, or inspired her to live differently. Countless thoughts raced through my mind as I thought about the tragedy of a young black woman losing the battle with her demons. It hurt because I too fought the same demons that she did. I fought the unwavering and cold-hearted spirit of addiction, and I knew that once it placed its claws on you, you would be fighting for your life to get them off of you.

"Damn..." I muttered. But my expression wasn't just because Black Barbee died. It was because I was losing everybody around me and everything I owned. My father, my artist, my child's mother, my wife, my money— The only things I had left were my health, my sanity, my faith, my kids, my freedom— I knew I needed to get my life together before I ended up literally losing it all for good.

"Yea, crazy right? But it gets worse..."

I really wasn't ready for more bad news, but I guess I had to face the world at some point. I'd turned my phone off for days and yet the world was still waiting on me as soon as I turned it right back on.

"Worse? Worse how?"

"Well... Since you forgot to sign the contract, it's invalid. Which means the royalties will be going to her next of kin, and in this case... there's an ex-boyfriend stating that she had a valid contract with him."

"What?" My anger was starting to rear its ugly head again. "What's the boyfriend's name?" There was the old me again, preparing to hurt someone— then I caught myself and exhaled. "You know... nevermind. I don't want it."

My lawyer was either surprised or angry, which one I didn't know, nor did I care. Gone were the days that I continued the perpetual cycle of pain— hurting the world only for the world to come back and hurt me in a different form.

"Devin you sure you don't want his name? I can get you his name and address so you can send... a postcard or something. He's literally the only thing separating your company from receiving the posthumous royalties from her music. It should be in the range of $7 million, maybe more since other popular artists have been making all these RIP posts for her."

I hung the phone up without responding. The devil had been making me all types of offers for my soul, and I was done unknowingly making deals with his ass. Now that I knew better— there was no way possible I was going back down that path again. I wanted growth. I wanted life. Love. Faith and healing. I turned my phone back off and placed it besides my wife's phone. I kept her phone charged the same way she used to keep it charged, and I carried it with me no matter where I went and I never ever had the urge to go through her phone, nor would I ever attempt.

Having her phone close to mine felt like old times. I loved that lady, and I was going to go to God every day until He saw enough change in me to bring her home to me.

TERRANCE

At my age, I was old enough to recognize my mistakes and flaws, even if I wasn't strong enough or smart enough to correct them. I was old and naïve, and I would probably die that way. I blame my past examples on my current collective set of traits. I watched my father be old and naïve, and I ignored all of the warnings the same way I watched my father ignore his warnings. I watched my father die in the streets, and I too tried to go out the way that he did; only that wasn't the plan that God had for me.

Maybe if my father had gone to prison, then he wouldn't have died in the streets. I was happy for the amount of time that I did have with my son, and I hoped that he saw the mistakes in me were the same flaws in him- and hoped that he would see that my path isn't the right path and make a change for the best. My son had status and power in this world, and he didn't even realize it. He had what me and my father did not have, and if he could realize his own power, he would have the opportunity to break a generational curse of anger and naivety.

I was going to die angry and naïve, but he didn't have to be as stupid as I was. I was unable to change because I was forever indebted to the rules of the streets. I'd took a gamble with Banny's information, and now that I was back in the penal system, I knew there was only a matter of time for when Banny's goons were going to strike. I wasn't going to pray to God for me, because I didn't deserve forgiveness. I knew that I was about to try to kill Banny before they killed me, and that's how I was going to leave this earth— with that same mindset.

The world has different types of people for a reason. Variety— the outsiders always criticized people like myself, but they didn't walk in our shoes, so they wouldn't understand. I lived in a dog eat dog world, and even when I wasn't hungry I still had to eat just so that I wouldn't be eaten. I didn't feel anything when I heard about Barbee's death. If anything I felt relieved, because if I was out there with her I probably would have died on the same batch of drugs.

The world operated in cycles. It operated in the name of penalty. Root word *penal*— so this was all I knew; the penal system and an eye for an eye. Justice back in my day meant that if somebody pushed me in grade school that I'd better had pushed them back or get a whooping from my mama. That's how I grew up, so that's what I put back out in the world. There was no such thing as being happy forever. It didn't matter your current level of success, and it didn't matter how much money you had— as long as you were living, you still had the burden of living.

Water fell, a plant grew, the plant died and a new plant grew in its place. Nobody remembers the plant that grew four generations before the current one, and nobody cared.

It didn't matter how pretty the flower was, it still got pulled.

DEVIN

There were only about 30 people in the church total, and it was the most amazing experience I'd had aside from marrying my wife and watching my first child come into this world. For our town, church attendance was much higher than the average major city. 30 people out of 2,000 attending this church alone meant that over 1% of the entire population was present. I sat beside my Uncle in the third row as I watched my Aunty handle a few miscellaneous things within the church.

She was an usher, and had been an usher for over 60 years faithfully. Her loyalty was amazing, and she not only showed it with her church, but also to her husband and her family. She was an unwavering portrait of strength. I sat in silence waiting for the pastor to come out to speak, and in the silence I couldn't help but to hear my Uncle struggle with his breathing.

"You good Unc?" I said as I touched his hand.

His throat constricted and and he looked at me startled. "Yea. Yes. I'm ok."

"You sure?"

"I'm as good as I'll ever be."

When the pastor came out, my eyes almost popped out of my face. It was my childhood friend, Benjamin.

Benjamin? I couldn't believe it. That man had ran through so many women in high school, I'm surprised he had the courage to even walk in a church.

My Uncle smiled when he saw my reaction. "That's your old buddy ain't it?" He laughed gently, and it seemed like a struggle for him to express himself. "Don't worry, he's one of the best preachers we done ever heard preach."

I nodded my head silently. I know Benjamin saw me, but he didn't make a big deal out of it. I could tell he was focused and was a man on a mission. To hear my Uncle at his age call Benjamin one of the best was shocking. I was intrigued.

"Forgiveness." His words echoed through the small church, causing me to take a deep breath. It was one of my main flaws.

"Times... We got the nerve to ask God... for forgiveness, and every time we ask, He forgives. Then... When someone wrongs us, we're mad. We don't wanna forgive but we want it done to us. Did you know that you're not perfect? Let me tell you something... I've been married to my wife for 7 years now. She's one of the reasons for me being here today. God sent me her. But guess what y'all? I have morning breath, and she forgives me."

A few people laughed as he started to get deeper in his sermon.

"My feet ugly and she forgives me. I'm not tall like a basketball player and I don't look like a model, and she forgives me. My wife is beautiful y'all. I know she can find somebody taller, better looking, more money, a person who makes less mistakes than me... But guess what? She's right here. I make a mistake without even realizing it sometimes. I just do the craziest stuff sometimes, and she still forgives me.

God is a forgiving God. We can't ask for forgiveness if we can't forgive. We can't break the chains of the past, or move on from our mistakes if we can't forgive. When God made us... He knew He'd made a beautiful mess. To make up for the mess that we were about to make out here, He had to add something called Forgiveness to the recipe. See... forgiveness doesn't mean go intentionally do the wrong thing and ask for forgiveness. That's not asking for forgiveness, that's asking God to accept an insult.

Forgiveness. I didn't intend to hurt you, please forgive me. I didn't mean to do what I did, please forgive me. Or... I recognize that what I did was wrong, and I won't do it anymore, please forgive me. Not... I keep hitting you in the face, please forgive me today and I do it again tomorrow. Forgiveness and insult is different."

I listened to a beautiful sermon, and left church that night carrying valuable lessons with me. I was going to fast for seven days, and pray each day in the place of my hunger. I was only going to drink tall glasses of water when I was hungry, and eat once per day. I couldn't wait to get back to my Aunt and Uncle's house so I could get on my knees and pray. Even though I didn't have much money left, I felt my burdens become lighter as my mentality changed. I didn't wanna hurt anymore– meaning I didn't wanna feel pain or deliver it. I didn't desire to be on either side of the coin of pain.

☙❧

Three days of fasting had me weak and barely able to move. My energy was lower each day, but whatever energy I had left I gave it to God. I was on my knees with my hands clasped and my spirit open.

"God please go to work in me. Deliver me from my demons and make me whole again. Help me to be a better me. I don't want to hurt anymore God please. I ask that you take this depression away, take my addictions away, take my anger away– guide me so that I can guide others. God please take the pain away from the ones I love, remove the hate out of my heart so I can give more love to the ones that I love. I need you God. Protect my family through this journey– wrap your arms around us and keep us out of harm's way."

DEVIN

I turned the light off and got in the small twin sized bed. It was hot in my Uncles and Aunt's trailer since their air conditioning didn't get that cool, and it was the middle of summer. I had the window open letting the cooler night air circulate the stuffy room. I listened to the crickets create a familiar song– the type of music that I could never be talented enough to create. I listened to the poems of the crickets, the consistent measurements of volume– symmetry in sound.

I was happy that my Uncle and Aunt had given me a place to stay without judging me. It meant the world to me and I vowed to repay them one day. The crickets continued to sing its song, and it wasn't long before the talented artists made me drop my guard and sang me into a slumber.

※

One of the deepest sounds of pain I'd ever heard came roaring through the room at around 5 in the morning. I jumped up startled, and didn't know if it was an animal being attacked outside or if it was on the inside. I heard the scream again, a gut-rattling, heart-pounding scream that was strong enough to rip through a bulletproof vehicle.

"Annieeeee!" It was my Uncle's voice, louder and deeper than I'd ever heard.

I jumped out of the bed and ran through the house to see what was going on, and stood stunned as I saw paramedics clamoring over her body. I was confused. I'd been sleeping while my Uncle and Aunty were suffering. My Uncle was crying, yelling, screaming, he was in real pain. I looked at my Aunty and it didn't look like she was breathing. She lay lifeless as the paramedics worked on her as best as they could. One of the nurses was trying to console my Uncle, but I knew that nothing was going to console him. She was everything he'd ever known, and after 60 plus years, she'd grown to become a piece of him and him the peace for her.

I didn't even realize I was crying until a nurse came over and handed me a napkin. "What happened?" I asked as I watched them put my Aunty's lifeless body on the stretcher and carry her to the ambulance.

"I'm sorry. She died in her sleep."

My Uncle fell to his knees, took his fist and slammed it on the floor repeatedly. "Annie noooo! Please don't leave me Annie! You can't leave me here like this! Please Anniieeeeeee! You're everything to me! Don't leave meeeeee! Don't leeeeaavveeee meeeeeee! Pleeeeeeeease!"

I turned and went to my room, my tears uncontrollable, my emotions on overload. I slipped on a t-shirt and shorts, put on a pair of sneakers and ran out the back door. There was a path I used to run through when I was a kid, and I had many memories of running that path when something hurt me. It was a path through the woods that went on for at least a 5 mile stretch.

I ran and cried.

Everytime my foot hit the ground I unleashed more pain out of my body.

Images of my Uncle crying after losing his wife, my Aunty- I'd never witnessed pain the depths of what I'd witnessed that morning.

My sweet Aunty. She didn't do anything to anyone, and was the nicest person I'd known. Not to mention she was one of the only older family members I had left on this earth. God had taken her from us, but what hurt more than that was the fact that I knew my Uncle's heart was broken. I ran for hours, ran until the morning sun came, and until I was beginning to get dehydrated.

I wasn't getting dehydrated from running, but instead I was losing all my liquid from crying. I'd been running for 2 hours before I turned around to head back. My body was exhausted, so I ran some of the way and walked some of the way. I was really thirsty, but I would be ok. When I passed a familiar point in my path, I knew that I wasn't far from the trailer so I started running faster. When I finally made it out of the path, I stopped and bent over to catch my breath. I was crying and trying to breath at the same time. I knew my Aunty was in a better place but I felt so bad for my Uncle.

I wiped my eyes as best as I could and stood up, only for the tears to fall harder.

My wife's car was parked in the yard, the sight of it nearly made my heart stopped.

A million emotions came over me, and none of them I was familiar with. I managed to get myself together and walked through the back door of the trailer. They didn't hear me and they never knew I was there. I took one step, and stopped when I heard them in deep conversation with my Uncle crying his heart out.

"That man loves you Ashlon! And I know you love him or you wouldn't have gon through all that trouble to find out where he was! You say you tracked a phone or something? That's love! I lost my wife of 60 plus years this morning, and I'm hear to tell you right now that every single moment I spent with her was worth it! All of our days were worth more than gold itself. You see... in 60 years of being married to the same person, it was a lot of arguments, disagreements, a lot of difficult times. Ego, attitudes, anger, silent treatments– but we still got through it all because we told God we were going to do that for each other. We don't lie to God. It hurts because I always thought I would leave this earth before she did."

My Uncle took a pause and cried harder. Undoubtedly my wife's tears were causing him to be more emotional, because it was getting to me as well.

"Ashlon... You gotta understand that it takes us men 11 years more than a woman does to reach emotional maturity. See... women reach emotional maturity at the age of 32, and that man doesn't reach it until 43 years of age. Emotional maturity... I'm talking about getting silent during arguments, that's emotional immaturity. Laughing when it's inappropriate, saying mean things teasing his woman and thinking it's ok. Emotional maturity and maturity are different in that one is only in regards to protecting the other person's feelings. The other type of maturity is often mistake for the real deal, when all that does is shows you that a person takes showers, puts on deodorant and brushes their teeth.

You gotta let that man become a man in order for him to become a man. What I mean by that... Becoming a man takes time. Don't believe the hype thinking just because a boy is a certain age that he's a man. No ma'am, a man becomes one when he seeks the deepest knowledge available of how to protect his woman from all types of harm including emotional, physical and spiritual. That's how I protected my Annie. I made sure she was free from all types of harm, but God just wanted to have her with him today."

I couldn't take it anymore. Listening to my Uncle's pain made me wanna take all the pain away from everyone I loved. I walked through the house and into the room where they were sitting. I saw her before she saw me, and she was more beautiful that moment than every other time except for our wedding day. When she saw me she jumped up and wrapped her arms around me as tight as she could. I was sweaty with a wet t-shirt on and she didn't care in the least bit.

"I'm so sorry Devin. I was only trying to be obedient to what God wanted from me! I didn't mean to hurt you! I didn't mean to abandon you, or leave you in your time of need! I'm sorry if I hurt you even for a second! I'm so sorry Devin! I just wanted to be obedient in what God asked of me. He woke me up in the middle of the night and put it on my heart to come to you. I didn't even know what your Uncle was going through, but I'm so sorry! I don't wanna live another moment without you Devin. Please forgive me."

I kissed her in response. It wasn't her that needed to be forgiven, it was me.

"You didn't do anything wrong Ashlon." I said through tears. "I love you even more today than I loved you then, and I didn't think that was possible. See now I love you with a clear conscience, and I want nothing more than to grow old with you. I love you Ashlon, but I need you to forgive me. I wanna be a man good enough to one day deserve a woman as good as you. I wanna show you how thankful I am, how appreciative of that you're in my life, and I never want us to separate again, not even for a moment. Being without you is the hardest thing I've ever had to endure in this lifetime, so please don't do that again."

We hugged.
We cried.
We both hugged my Uncle simultaneously.
He cried.
We cried.

Tears meant replacement. It was the flush of pain, weakness, and hurt with the presence of power. It was the process of washing away the difficult moments so that you could take in the better frames.

As a family, we were all we needed. Just us.

Money was ok, but family was better. Family is how you fought addiction, anger, and flaws. Family is how you were able to survive in such a cold-hearted world. Family is what pulled you through situations that a stranger would bury you in.

God.
Family.
Tears.

AUTHOR'S NOTE

Having money is less important than having peace.

I had my first bestselling e-book back in February 2011. The e-book game was just getting started, and I'd hit the urban fiction market selling my stories at the low price of 99 cents. I remember back then I used to argue a lot with authors because they kept telling me that I was undercutting and devaluing black literature. I didn't see it the same way because I was really just happy that people were paying anything at all to read my thoughts and stories. It was never my intention to try to get rich from books— I lived in my 2,000 population town at the time— Buena Vista, GA, so all it took for me to make it there was about $1,000 to $1,500 per month. That was honestly all I looked forward to making.

My 99 cent books sold more and more copies, until eventually there were authors asking for me to help them get their copies sold also. I was hesitant initially because I didn't feel like I would do a good job and I didn't wanna fail. I told them to let me build my name up a little first and I would get back with them. Around February 2012, I'd dropped yet another #1 e-book— this is a time period when it was rare to drop a #1 Urban Fiction e-book because

AUTHOR'S NOTE

the e-book game wasn't organized and was less crowded. I was approached again for assistance, but this time I decided to help.

Over the years I went from aiming to make $1,000 a month to months where I was making over $200,000 a month, and was as unhappy as I could possibly be. It wasn't unhappy because of the money, it was unhappy because of everything that came with it. I went through things with $200,000 that you couldn't have paid me $200,000 to do if I were dead broke. And with that logic, I completely walked away from my companies last year and started my life over.

It's never an easy transition going from making $200k a month to anything, but I found peace in the process. Besides, much like Devin, when I was making $200k a month, I'd developed a ridiculous gambling habit, so it wasn't like I had the $200k for long anyways. My addiction to Las Vegas' casinos were out of control. I wasn't gambling because I needed money, because all of my bills were paid. I was gambling because I was literally addicted. I had days where I would make $80,000 gambling starting with $5,000; and by the end of the week I would be down $120,000.

I earned 7-Star status in Las Vegas casinos, the highest gambling honor you could earn from Caesar's Palace– having at least a million dollars in wins touch my hand, yet I never kept the money and always gambled it back. My habit was a controlled habit, because I paid all of my bills for myself and my family first, and then the rest... well you know where the rest went. I never had to pay for rooms in Las Vegas because my 7-Star status gave them to me free of charge. I never paid for food, that was free too. Airfare, free, hell I could even tell them to give me a bonus, and they would pay me $1,000 cash to come to Caesar's Palace to gamble.

Free alcohol, a shopping mall connected to the casino, and free luxury suites as long as I wanted to stay– I was hooked.

However, while the big wins were nice and something to take pictures and video of... The big losses would lead me to deep depression. Can you imagine having $200,000 cash and then

AUTHOR'S NOTE

needing to budget a few thousand for the rest of the month because you went overboard? Thinking about if I had to do it again, I would– because I have an addictive personality, who knows what I would have been addicted to if it hadn't have been gambling?

I eventually walked away from owning so many publishing companies, leaving hundreds of thousands of dollars on the table and I started seeking happiness. It wasn't easy initially, but I made it work. I had a place that I was paying $10,000 a month for, and I let it go. For what? I lived alone, and that was just crazy anyways. I fought my depression and started fighting my way back against the things that held me down. My past. My demons and addictions. I started trying to clean my life up to the best of my ability, and that's when I mentally took myself back from trying to make all types of crazy amounts of money to trying to write the best stories I could write and hopefully help someone in the process.

That's when I wrote Broken Crayons Still Color, and I was nervous to put that book out because I was afraid of what people would say. I put it out anyways, and sad to say it... alcohol helped me not worry about what people would say... Next thing I knew, that was my best-selling book of my career. As of the time of me writing this author note, Broken Crayons Still Color has 1,000 reviews in the span of 5 months. So basically a lot of people had plenty to say, and I'm so appreciative.

It's those 1,000 reviews that pulled me out of my depression and helped me get my life back together emotionally, spiritually, mentally, and creatively. It's those reviews that made me start finding land to buy in my small hometown, build my dream home and keep writing stories for my supporters. It's those reviews that brought me my happiest moments whenever I found myself going through an emotional slump or found myself feeling down and out. It's those reviews that helped me go from drinking hard liquor everyday, mixing it with pills of all types... to simply drinking a red wine every now and then.

It's those reviews that changed my life, and if you are one of

AUTHOR'S NOTE

the people who left me a review for Broken Crayons Still Color, then I am so thankful that God used you to talk to me. I'm a Taurus so I am a bit hard-headed, but it's hard to ignore when people are speaking to me in volume. I know I always say this, but I truly want you to understand how much those reviews meant to me.

A broken spirit who just wanted to heal but didn't see a way. It was you who returned my energy with your words. You matched my prayers with your prayers and I just thank you so much for being a part of my healing and growth.

I had some deeper personal stuff that I'd considered adding to this author note, but I'm really tired of crying, so I'll go ahead and wrap this one up; and the deeper stuff I need to continue to sort through until the timing is right.

Thank you for supporting me, just a flawed small town guy trying his best to be the best version of himself as he could possibly be. Just a small town guy learning what forgiveness means and learning how to detach the chains locking me down to the hurt of my past. I recognize that I still have a long way to go, but the devil has to recognize now that I'm no longer falling for his stupid tricks. Healing is a beautiful process. To an outsider, all they see is a fresh scab and it looks bad, but to the person wearing the scab, they're excited about the new growth.

Thank you.

P.S. Thank you for leaving reviews and showing love on Amazon for Broken Crayons Still Color. I enjoyed reading your letters and hearing your advice and opinions. I'll be looking for your replies again this time for part 2.

Blessings and love to my #DavidReaders
David Weaver

STAY UP TO DATE

FOLLOW ME ON IG: @theRealRichForever

Subscribe to my mailing list: TBRS to 95577

Made in the USA
Middletown, DE
09 September 2025

17300330R00138